# Is This a Joke?

by

Robert G. Simmons, Jr.

**DORRANCE PUBLISHING CO., INC.**
**PITTSBURGH, PENNSYLVANIA 15222**

ISBN # 0-8059-4233-5
Printed in The United States of America

*First Printing*

For information or to order additional books, please write:
Dorrance Publishing Co., Inc.
643 Smithfield Street
Pittsburgh, Pennsylvania 15222
U.S.A.

From: Fred Burner, Publisher
To: Gary K. Live, Editor.

Prepare an article on survival and prosperity of the world. Analyze. Present solutions. Have ready for publication in thirty days. Do not interrupt any pending projects.

"Is this a joke?"Gary Live said to himself after finding and reading this memo on his desk in the editorial offices of the Daily Record, the only daily newspaper in his city.

Gary had learned early in life-long before he had started working for Fred Burner and Burner's newspaper-that when the job to be done was "impossible," that meant you had to do it yourself. Doing what the memo requested, within that time limit, at first glance looked impossible. Therefore, Gary thought this must be a joke of Fred Burner's, the owner and publisher of the paper. Before dismissing the matter as a joke, Gary considered how he was going to do what his boss had ordered. He concluded he would have to do this himself.

Notwithstanding the advantage of "doing it himself,"Gary knew immediately that when he had completed what he had been asked to do there would probably be doubt and disagreement among the paper's readers. What he would write would not result in any solution or agreement. It would result in answers which were controversial. Gary understood that writing an objective solution to any one of the factors of the world's survival or prosperity, by himself in thirty days without putting off what else he was doing, was "impossible." He knew immediately he had to have some help from someone who might think differently than he, i.e., someone who could and would take the other side of a possibly controversial issue, a devil's advocate, so to speak, an adversary.

Gary realized that the person he needed to help him do this job would have to be a friendly adversary-if there could be such a thing as a friendly adversary.

While contemplating the problems of this new assignment and the persons in the department who might be helpful, Gary noticed Ann Lawyer, one of the very best writers on the staff, racing down the aisle outside of his office as if she was late for something. Ann was in a hurry as if she had some important place to go with something important to do.

Gary wondered why he had not thought of Ann right away as the friendly adversary. She was smart and energetic. She wrote in an interesting way even on dull subjects. She seemed to like whatever she did regardless of how short or how long or how complicated the assignment might be. In fact Gary knew Ann was smarter and a better writer than he. Gary knew that if he had not been employed first, Ann Lawyer would probably have his job now.

Would Ann be a good friendly adversary? Gary did not know if she was friendly or, for that matter, if she could be friendly. Ann always seemed congenial to the other employees. To be honest, Gary had to admit to himself that Ann and he had not ever had a friendly conversation or discussed anything that did not pertain to work to be done.

One Monday morning Gary had run into Ann in the aisle next to her desk when no others on the staff had yet arrived for work. For reasons Gary could not explain, he had said, "You look happy this morning."

Ann turned with a pleasant smile and with a charming voice replied, "Well, thank you. I am happy this morning."

Ann killed the conversation right there, leaving Gary with the intriguing question as to what she had done over the weekend that made her appear to be so happy. Gary had not done anything himself for a long time that had made him as happy as Ann seemed to be.

Gary had let the conversation die. They both had gone about their business. It did not take long to observe that Ann seemed happy every morning and every afternoon, too.

Gary concluded Ann could adopt the posture of an adversary to him, regardless of her personal inclinations on possible controversial solutions. But Ann was a woman. It had never occurred to Gary he could write something as a co-author with a lady. Was he prejudiced or chauvinistic, or was he so shy because he had never known a woman well enough to think about working closely with one?

There was one thing Gary knew. If he was prejudiced or chauvinistic, such inclination would show in the final article. A lady would be a balancing adversary to make the final result look fair. Ladies were part of the world. They were an ever-increasing force in both the work place and government. Having a lady involved might give a different (perhaps a better) perspective to the problems of survival and prosperity. A lady might reach different conclusions than Gary would. It would be hard to work with a lady, Gary thought. For some feeling (not reason), Gary felt nervous about Ann.

Gary knew he could bite the bullet. He could get this project done with Ann if she would work with him. After all, it was for only thirty days.

Getting Ann involved required some planning.

Gary first thought of picking up the office telephone intercom and asking Ann to come to his office. Why he hesitated to do this puzzled Gary. Was he afraid she would say no? Or was he afraid she would say yes? Certainly Gary did not want to start out by saying, "Will you be my friendly adversary?"

Gary had noticed Ann was not like the other women working at the paper. Her clothes were never too tight. Her skirts were never too short, although Gary did not know when a dress was too tight or a skirt was too short or too long. Gary had noticed Ann did not wear earrings, but then that was practical because she used the telephone so often.

Gary could not tell if Ann wore makeup. He had never been close enough to her to see. If she did wear makeup, she wore it so carefully she just looked healthy, or if she did not wear makeup, she must be healthy. She sure looked healthy and happy.

He had noticed that there was no ash tray on her desk.

Gary wondered why these thoughts were coming to his mind when he should be working. He knew, or felt, his approach to Ann had to be made carefully. Gary decided to avoid the phrase "friendly adversary." Ann might think the whole idea was a gag or a gimmick to start something else. After all, this was work. It should be approached as work not as a friendly endeavor on company time.

Rolling a pink memo sheet into his old manual typewriter, Gary pecked out:

Interoffice Memo
From: Gary K. Live, Editor
To: Ann Lawyer

Fred Burner has assigned a project which may be interesting. At your convenience, please drop into my office so we may discuss this matter. Do not interrupt your present activity.

Rolling the memo out of the typewriter, Gary took a quick look at what he had typed. He took a quicker look through the glass wall of his office to the open work area which housed the newspaper staff. Ann's chair was empty. Gary made a quick trip to her desk. He placed the memo on top of her glasses, which were lying on top of a stack of notes of some kind. Gary did not pause long enough to discover what Ann's present activity might have been. He did not want anyone who happened to glance that way to think he was snooping. It was very unusual for him to have been looking at anyone's desk. In fact, it was unusual for Gary to have been in the area at all. He made a quick return to his own office.

Ann was in the file area jokingly called the "library." There a computer would bring up on the screen the dates and a summary of the substance of any matter discussed in the paper after the computer was installed. It would also bring up a lot of other materials which had not been published, assuming the correct buttons were pushed. Ann knew just what she wanted to find. She also knew which buttons to push to get what she needed. When Ann turned the machine on, she reached to find her glasses where she usually kept them, in her hair. It was convenient to carry them there.

Ann did not park her glasses there just to look nice. She needed her glasses when she read, wrote, or looked at the computer screen. Ann, in fishing in her hair, could not find her glasses. She stopped to think about what she had done with them. She remembered she had decided to quit wearing them in her hair because that smudged them, and they needed cleaning so often. She thought she must have left the glasses on her desk. It was a waste of time to go back to her desk to get them, but she would have to have them to get the data she wanted. Hurrying back to her desk for her glasses was a chore. Ann pounded her heels on the terrazzo floor even harder than usual. When she approached her desk, Ann could not see the glasses. Had she left them some place else, or had she lost them?

While trying to recall where the glasses might be, Ann saw the pink memo sheet on her desk. It had not been there when she had gone to the library. A quick squint at the slip would satisfy her curiosity. She went to her desk. Without sitting down, she picked up the memo, squinted, and saw her glasses.

With one graceful movement, she put on her glasses, sat down, and read the note.

Ann was surprised. She wondered why Gary had sent her a note instead of calling her on the intercom. How did the memo get there? Had Gary brought it himself? Had Gary deliberately arranged to bring the memo when Ann was not there? If so, why?

Ann had often wondered about Gary. He seemed congenial to all of the people who worked at the paper. He worked long hours and hard. He did not seem to expect the others to work that long or that hard. As far as Ann could tell, Gary was a bore because he had only talked about business except that one Monday morning when Gary surprised her by saying, "You look happy this morning."

Ann remembered she had thought that for once perhaps he was trying to start a conversation. Ann had kicked herself several times for letting the conversation drop by merely replying, "Why, thank you. I am happy this morning." Gary had said no more. Ann had almost chased him to keep the conversation going, but Gary had gone on. The occasion had ended.

Having daydreamed more than was her habit, Ann read the pink memo.

What did it mean? Was it something Gary had thought up just to start a conversation? Had Burner asked for something to be done that Gary would not or could not do by himself? Ann could not remember any time Gary had asked anyone to help him.

All of this self-questioning had destroyed the train of thought Ann had had when she had gone to the library. Looking across the area of the desks through the glass walls of Gary's office, she could see Gary at his desk. From this angle it appeared he was alone.

Ann decided she might just as well learn what Gary had in mind even though the pink memo said not to interrupt her present activity. It was already interrupted.

Ann usually walked around the office with her glasses off. This time she left them on. She wondered if she was timid about going to Gary's office. Perhaps the glasses were a shield or protection, but she had no idea what there was to shield or to protect.

In walking over to Gary's office, Ann noticed she did not pound her heels on the floor as hard as usual. Was she walking slower than usual, or was it that when she pounded the floor she knew what she was doing and her objective, while now she had no idea of what she was doing or of her objective? Ann did not even have any certainty as to what her feelings were or whether her objective was business or personal.

Passing by the glass wall of another office, Ann noticed in the glass reflection that her hair was as neat as it was when she had left her apartment this morning. All of her attire seemed to be where and how it belonged. Ann did not usually notice such things after she started to work. She wondered why she noticed them now.

As Ann approached Gary's office an usual sensation affected her. Was it anticipation? She thought to herself that if it was anticipation, it was time to find out and to get at it, whatever "get at it" meant.

Gary was looking down at something on his desk as Ann entered the office. Ann remained standing. Ann was about the same height as Gary's mother, which was about one foot shorter than Gary. Ann's posture and shape were just what Gary used to think of as beautiful when he was in high school. Ann was wearing a plain white blouse, a knee length brown skirt without a belt, and shoes which had heels about half as high as some high heels would be.

Ann started what would turn out to be a new adventure with the formal statement, "Mr. Live, did you send for me?"

Gary looked up. He suddenly wished he had put on a clean shirt this morning. His response was just as formal. He said, "Yes, I asked you to come to discuss a new assignment. Sit down."

Ann sat in the hard chair nearest the desk. She leaned back a little in the chair. She crossed her legs. She noticed that with her glasses on she could not read the upside down papers on Gary's desk. She also noticed Gary's face was slightly blurred through the reading glasses. Without thinking, off came the glasses, which Ann then placed in her blouse pocket with a movement which disclosed there was something under the blouse.

Gary noticed the movement and the disclosure. He said to himself, "I wish she would not cross her legs."He noticed this brought her skirt up higher than he was used to seeing a skirt. This movement disclosed that Ann had at least one knee, something which had never occurred to Gary before.

As Ann had sat down, Gary had observed the movement of the glasses and the knee. He picked up the Fred Burner memo which had started all of this, handed the memo to Ann, and said, "My first impression on reading this when I got it was that it was one of Burner's jokes. Burner could not expect anyone to comply with such a request in thirty days and continue their regular work."

Before Ann had a chance to say anything, Gary said, "The subject is so all-inclusive. It, in effect, directs that I determine the factors involved in survival and prosperity, analyze the factors, and solve the problems of the world. I doubt if ten times the number of people we have on our staff could do something credible in a year. I decided it had to be a joke. I put in on my desk. I forgot about it until I returned this morning, when I was reminded of it because there it was on the desk staring at me."

"An assignment like that would confuse me, too," Ann said.

Gary continued, "In looking at Burner's memo again, I thought maybe it was not a joke. Maybe Burner wanted someone to give that subject a good try. I decided if doing what Burner requested was as impossible as it seemed, I would have to do it myself. I thought it would not be fair to ask someone else to do this. I decided to humor Burner and bring some disconnected thoughts on this subject together. That is what I decided to do although I still think it is probably a joke. Miss Lawyer, what do you think it is?"

"Now, Mr. Live-if you want to start this out on a last name basis-I have just seen this. My first impression is Mr. Burner does not joke about anything this profound. I think he wants you to do exactly what he said. I do not think it is just a joke."

Ann immediately realized she had just disagreed with Gary in their first conversation. It occurred to her this was not a good tactic for opening a discussion or in dealing on a personal basis with a man, although she had no experience which told her how to get along with a man. She also had not realized she cared about such things. So to repair any damage she had caused in disputing Gary, Ann made a quick effort to continue the conversation. Ann said, "You have just told me you had decided to do this yourself. Is that what you wanted of me, to ask me if I agreed with you that this is a little joke, or did you want me to help you on this?"

Without thinking about it, Ann now realized she had opened something that could last awhile, while at the same time she had deliberately injected herself into the possibility of some kind of activity with Gary.

Gary thought to himself that approaching Ann to participate in this was going to be easier than he had thought.

"Miss Lawyer, you are very perceptive. My thought was not that you would help me. My idea was that we would do this project together. I have concluded that one person cannot adequately do this. There is room for much genuine disagreement on this subject. There is possibly a significant amount of emotional turmoil in this subject, too."

"You are right. This probably involves the environment. Some people get very emotional when discussing the environment. I interpret Burner's subject to include environmental and other matters."

Gary replied with, "There is more than one side to almost every part of the problem. I know, roughly, what some of my thoughts are, but I am not sure I am right. I decided I could not do an objective analysis without someone to deliberately dispute my ideas, punch holes in them, and present his or her own ideas for me to deliberately dispute. In other words, to be adversaries."Gary almost said "friendly adversaries" but decided it was too early to use the "friendly" terminology. "So, I appreciate your suggestion of helping me to do this, but if I am thinking correctly, it cannot be just help; it has to be a joint activity. It has to be joint but always disagreeing until we..." Gary noticed he had used "we" ... "arrive at some conclusion which is the product of being adversaries."

Ann noticed Gary had used the term "disagreeing." It immediately occurred to her that if she, or they, were careful, "disagree" did not have to become "disagreeable." If Gary wanted her to disagree and dispute him to check to see he had not made a mistake in his thinking, Ann could and would do that. That meant also Gary would probably disagree with her and dispute her ideas.

Despite this purpose and division of labor, Ann thought she would be careful not to disagree any more than absolutely necessary to do a good job on the project. She would be careful. Ann did not want to be disagreeable. It was her nature to be happy with everyone. Certainly she did not want to be disagreeable with Gary. The happy thought was that Gary wanted the two of them to do this together. She asked herself, "Why did he ask me to be his devil's advocate?"

While these thoughts came to Ann, she did not say anything, but Gary continued with what he had been saying. "You may be wondering why I asked you to be the one to dispute me and for me to dispute you. Frankly, I have not known you well enough to know if you have any preconceived ideas on any part of the subject of Burner's memo or whether your preconceived ideas are the opposite of mine. All of the work you have done here for this paper has been so factual and objective that I have never observed any of your personal opinions showing in your work."

It occurred to Ann that perhaps she did not want to be an adversary with Gary, but she knew now she did want to do this project. She did want to do something with Gary. If disagreeing was a necessary part of working together, she would learn to disagree.

Ann also knew she did not know Gary's ideas well enough to even guess what side of any matter she would have to be on to disagree with him. Ann did not know if working together would require her to take a position which she opposed. Doubt and opportunity are not compatible, so opportunity prevailed.

"Mr. Live, it occurs to me that I do not know your ideas, either, or whether they are in conflict with mine. I believe that, as true objective reporters, we can adopt a position and advocate it objectively, carefully, and skillfully, without regard to our personal preconceived opinions. So I would like to work with you."

Ann, after having said that, thought the words she had used had two meanings: she would like to work on this project, and she would like to work with Gary. She realized she meant both of those meanings.

"Well, I appreciate your answer. It will be a tough job, but it should be interesting. Since I do not know your present ideas, and you do not know mine, what would you suggest as to the mechanics of getting this done on time?"

"I have not had time to think about this. The matter is completely new to me."

"You are correct. That was not a fair question for me to ask since you have just heard of this."

"Let me think about this for a while."

"What do you think of this? Since both of us have other things we have already started, and since they have to be completed while we work on this, each of us should spend the mornings completing our present assignments. We can spend the afternoons on our new project. As we finish our present assignments, we can then dedicate all of each day to Burner's memo until this project is completed."

Ann said, "I would guess that both of us are not going to finish our present work at the same time. Splitting each day seems like a good plan."

"Can we start this afternoon? For myself, I estimate I can finish or arrange to reassign to someone else what I am working on so that by the day after tomorrow I think I could spend most of my time on our project."

Gary wondered why he had used the word "our."

Ann could see this meeting was coming to an end. For some reason or feeling, she was not quite ready to close the matter. This conversation and project seemed to be getting more interesting.

"Are you and I going to do this alone? If so, I do not think we have the time to do any independent new research. We will probably have to accept the research done by others without verifying it ourselves. In doing this we"-"My goodness,"Ann thought, "I used the word "we."-"could make some mistakes. I think both of us"-"I did it again. I used the word "us" this time.- "I have enough perspective that if either of us"Again! "suspects someone else's research, we can avoid any serious errors."

Ann continued, "My first impression is any new research done by anyone else here at the paper would get in our way. There already is, I think, a lot of research on the subjects which are probably involved. I suggest we try it alone, just the two of us, until we find that will not work."

Ann was surprised at herself for being so assertive without having thought about these things at all.

Gary was also surprised Ann had such ideas so quickly. Gary hesitated. Perhaps Ann was a take-over person who would consciously or unconsciously chart the course and run things. She was beginning to sound a little bossy. Gary had not expected Ann to be bossy. He was not sure he wanted to work with someone who would be taking charge or wanted to be in charge. It had been his habit to be in charge. Before Gary started to say anything about who was to be in charge, he hesitated. He immediately saw that to make this project work, he could not be the sole boss. Leadership would have to be shared. Perhaps Ann was a leader who would not want to share the decisions.

Too late now. The project had to be done. He had already asked Ann. There was no one else who was smart enough or with whom he felt he wanted to work.

Gary said, "I had not thought things through that far. My first idea was that if this was not a joke and it had to be done in such a short time, I would not tell anyone I was using the research and ideas of others. I would not announce I had not verified their research. You know, Miss Lawyer, we might do a better job if we are not confused with facts."

"This is too serious to make into a joke."

"You are correct. I am not very funny. We will do this alone. There will be just the two of us involved."

"I like that idea."

"Burner sent this memo to me. I do not think anyone else knows anything about it. It would not help us to be objective if others knew and started to lobby us for their points of view. I suggest we keep this as our secret for now."

"That is a good idea, but someone in the office will notice we are spending a lot of time together. They will guess the wrong answer. They might think something other than office work is involved. Frankly that does not bother me if it does not bother you."

"Nothing bothers me if this job gets done on time with our usual high quality work. I do not care what other people think about me."

"Mr. Live, what do you suggest as to the mechanics of getting this project done?"

"We can use the empty glass-walled office down the hall from this office. The other employees will see us. They will be able to see we are working. There is a double desk with space to work while facing each other. You will want to use the word processor at your desk, or we can move it into that office. My guess is we will want to do our writing at our present desks. We can use the new office for discussions, proofing, rewriting, and being adversarial."

"We can start that way. If it does not work, we can change."

"My mother always taught me 'ladies first.' I have the habit of thinking 'ladies first.' That does not mean I think women are weaker or deserve more respect. My mother said, 'ladies first' because her parents taught her that kind of life. I mention this because I do not think we should regard each other as being different. You may have to humor me by letting me follow my mother's directions."

Ann was pleasantly surprised. Here was an old-fashioned sentimental guy who pretended to be tough. Ann liked that. She said, "Ladies first. I have not heard that expression for so long that I thought the term had disappeared in the women's liberation movement. I will accept whatever you do that is consistent with equality between men and women, without attaching any intent to it. But do not treat me as if you think women are inferior. I will not tolerate that."

There were a lot of things Ann could have said about men and women. There were some things she thought about briefly that were more concerned with herself and Gary personally, but she decided she had already said enough. Gary was all business.

"Time is limited. We have to get at this soon. I suggest we get started on this project right after lunch break today."

Ann smiled to herself. Already Gary had forgotten "ladies first." He was taking over the making of the decisions without consulting with her as he should in a joint matter. Gary was the boss. This time she should follow. There would be enough opportunities to disagree. This was not one of them.

"Agreed. I should be able to put to bed the story I am working on by noon. I will meet you at the glass-walled office at one o'clock."

All of this conversation had not taken even thirty minutes although Gary felt it had lasted longer. Gary also had the feeling this meeting had ended too soon.

Gary could not help noticing Ann's graceful turn as she arose from the chair and walked away as if she were dancing. In an instant Ann was out of sight.

Gary felt relieved things had gone so easily. He was having trouble getting back to thinking about whether he had planned anything for this morning.

Ann, as she walked to her desk, did not pound her heels on the hall tile. Her thoughts seemed to hold each foot up in the air. She wondered if she had been too abrupt in her departure. The whole meeting with Gary had moved so smoothly without preparation or contemplation that she was stunned. This might turn out to be something good she had not planned. Ann was not used to things happening which she had not planned.

Gary, not having any deadline or any special chores this morning, was unable to turn his thoughts from the project. He pushed away thoughts of Ann. He thought about getting the project done on time.

Gary thought Ann and he would have to be adversaries, but which side should she take? Which side should he take? For that matter, there would have to be a decision on what factors should be considered at all. How should the matters be written up after any conclusion was reached? Who would be the draftsman? These were subjects which they should discuss first.

Burner's memo should be the starting point. Gary read the memo again. They were to write on "The survival and prosperity of the world."

Gary now saw that the first matter they would have to determine was what factors should be included. They would then have to work out a solution to the problems of survival and prosperity.

A lot of thoughts came to Gary's mind. "Are there any problems in the world which do not fit under survival or prosperity? Do peace and war come within the scope of Burner's memo? With the modern ability to destroy, does not war and peace come under the subject of survival? Wars are expensive and cause economic confusion. That affects prosperity. Why are there wars?"

These might all be within the scope of Burner's memo. To answer even one of these would take more than thirty days. They would not be able to completely analyze all of these.

Should peace, war, and economic advancement be suggested to Ann as something which should be considered as factors?

*Is this too deep for Burner or our readers?* Gary thought, *Perhaps considering the subject at all is too deep for me but maybe not too deep for Ann.*

One o'clock looked like the start of an interesting time. One o'clock just might as well hurry up and come.

While waiting for one o'clock, Ann busied herself in completing what she had been doing when she had gone to the library. This did not succeed in pushing from her mind the memo from Burner.

What an inclusive question Burner had assigned! Did Burner include so much by accident? Did he expect the answer to the assignment to be solved in thirty days? Or did Burner intend this as a joke as Gary had at first thought?

Ann knew she had the ability to take a deep subject and so word her writing that, when it was presented, it did not look or sound deeper than the reader could comprehend. This was the ability which Ann thought was her best. Burner had not asked her to do this. Burner had not yet recognized her skill.

The memo of Burner was directed specifically to Gary K. Live. Did Burner want Gary to do this alone? Ann knew Gary also had the ability to write about a complex matter simply enough that anyone would understand it. Ann thought perhaps Gary was better at this than she.

Ann had some, but not very many, preconceived notions. Being the only child of a man who had wanted a son, Ann had been coached to know she could do anything better than any other girl and could do anything which did not require size or strength better than any boy. Generally this was true. Ann was good in women's sports, but women's sports no longer appealed to Ann. The competition was not aggressive enough.

Ann enjoyed a good book more than a good game. Her taste in music ran away from the loud. She loved to dance. The boys had loved to dance with her. Ann had never had any special boyfriend.

Ann had been worrying about the future of her job. It paid enough. There were interesting things to do. She wondered if she wanted to spend the rest of her life doing this. This new project suddenly looked like the beginning of a long highway to something better.

Ann prized her attitude of having no preconceived notions on anything. She knew she actually did have some preconceived ideas. She also knew she could decide each matter on its own merits as each problem arose.

Ann knew that was a good attitude to have. She was not sure that was what Gary had in mind when he had had said he wanted Ann to be an adversary. Ann guessed she could be an adversary. Perhaps all he meant was that she was to examine Gary's ideas to see if they followed logically and consistently from the data he would work up, not that she was to pick holes in his ideas or draftsmanship or be a fault finder.

Even though Ann had been given assignments concerning spousal abuse, child abuse, malnutrition, and poor housing, she was not dominated by the thought that it was her place as a journalist to change the world. Her job was to get the facts and then to report the facts.

Ann had realized there was a reason why some but not all of the poor people in the world were, in fact, poor. She thought some of them would continue to be poor no matter what the government or some social agency might do for them. She also wondered if it were not true that some of the poor she had met could get out of poverty if they had been given the attention, affection, encouragement, and help from someone as she had received from her father.

At one time Ann had considered becoming a teacher so she would be in the position to help someone who needed that kind of help. At one time Ann had also considered becoming a nurse or a social worker. She now realized she had decided to become a writer so her ideas could be seen and heard. She had thought perhaps she could accomplish more this way.

Ann had read about the problems of the poor. She had interviewed many poor people. Was being poor a factor which should be included in Burner's assignment?

Ann had read about the problems of the environment. She had never personally experienced anything serious. She had observed the exhaust smell of the trucks and busses on the streets. Ann did not like the smell of the smoke filled restaurants where she went occasionally with her friends. She knew a little about air and water pollution. She had some ideas about the cost and expense of cleaning up the air and the water.

Ann knew of the problem of destroying the green areas of the world, the forests, and the plants in order to make more paved streets, parking lots, and areas to build, homes, stores, and factories. Ann could see that people who did a lot of this destruction of the environment were, in fact, thinking they were improving their own prosperity. Ann could see that paying the cost and expense of curing the environment required prosperity. Not doing some of these things would weaken prosperity.

She realized there was a connection between survival and prosperity. Each required the other.

One o'clock just might as well hurry up and come.

# CHAPTER TWO

As it had always done once every day for ages, one o'clock did come.

Ann intended to be in the glass walled office first. Gary saw her coming. They arrived at the door at the same time. There was no room for both to enter together even if they both turned sideways. Gary surrendered. He followed. This was "ladies first."

Ann had two pads of lined note paper and six pencils. Gary had two pencils and two pads.

Without saying a word they both sat down, Ann with her back to the glass wall while Gary faced Ann and the whole staff, who had either not noticed them meeting this way or did not care.

They both started to talk at the same time. Again Gary yielded. It was ladies first again. Ann said, "We are to discuss what affects the survival and prosperity of the world. I suppose that means we start out by itemizing the factors of survival and prosperity in order to find the significant factor in each or both that we will wish to discuss. Survival and prosperity are either two subjects, or it is one subject with two aspects which are interrelated and have to be expressed together."

"Yes."

"Gary." First name now. "What do you think?"

"I consider that Burner was thinking of survival and prosperity as being one subject. I suspect, however, it will be easier to write this assignment if we start as if they were two subjects, analyze each, and then try to tie them together. Perhaps we can start one way and see how things work out. If that does not feel or sound right, we can always rewrite if we have the time."

"I seem to spend my life rewriting. I suspect this will be the same. I kind of like the idea of starting out fresh on something which has so few boundaries."

Gary continued, "If they are actually two subjects or two aspects of the same subject or two perspectives or two approaches, we can work separately. We should bear in mind they are probably parts of the same matter and will have to be coordinated."

Ann waited for Gary to go on. He did.

"If my first impressions are correct, any solution to any factor of survival is going to be expensive to accomplish. The solution to that problem will cost so much and affect so many people there will have to be prosperity to pay the expenses. Then on the other hand, we cannot have prosperity all over the world if the world is not going to survive somewhat as we know it now." Gary paused, before going on.

"Perhaps this is a 'which came first, the chicken or the egg' problem. Survival and prosperity are together. Success in working out a solution for one will depend on success in working out a solution for the other. I do not think we should think of this as if it were two subjects."

Ann asked herself, "Do Gary and I think alike, or is the fact that survival and prosperity are parts of the same thing so obvious that we both naturally came to this same conclusion?"

What Ann said was, "I do not think it would work out very well if both of us went at this as if the two subjects were the same. It appears to me that with the limited time we have, we should each work on part as if it were the only part. When each of us has finished a part, we can then tie them together. At that time we should work together on both parts at the same time."

Gary noticed the "work together" comment. He was not disappointed. He did not want the conversation to die on that, so he carried on with, "We probably ought to start on one, go through that one and find the significant factors, and then go on to the other. Have you ever tried anything like this?"

"Well, yes and no. I have never worked on anything so broad and all-inclusive as this before. I have worked on both sides of a problem. Sometimes I have made more or less alternate discussions with myself of each side of the problem in order to keep perspective. When I did this I got all my information together first, looked at it, and then decided how to balance the parts. I wanted to see if they were complementary to or opposite of each other. Perhaps we are doing what my father used to call 'getting the cart before the horse.' That is certainly an obsolete expression. We do not use either carts or horses any more, but you know what I mean. I suspect we had better find out what we think before we decide how to say what it is we think."

Gary was a little surprised at that suggestion, but he supposed it was correct on this project because he, at least, had no idea yet as to what to say about that broad subject Burner had assigned. Gary, without thinking it out fully, then said, "Let's each compile a list of what we think are factors involved in survival and then compile another list of factors involved in prosperity. Then we can see how they fit and relate to each other. Then we can decide which factors we should objectively analyze."

"I have already started such a list."

"So have I."

"Once we have our ideas in mind, we can then divide up the writing chores, or do you think we should do this all together?"

"No, Gary, you are correct when it comes to getting the ideas on paper, but I think, just as you said this morning, we should take different views on various aspects until we have a consensus. Then either of us could write our view."

Gary now followed with, "I suspect if one of us did all the writing, the final draft would read better than with two different styles of writing not fitting together.

We do not have time to do that. Perhaps we can make our writing styles fit in a revision upon which each of us should work."

Ann liked the idea of all of the writing being done together although she realized that not much would get done in the writing if each sentence was the product of both of them. She said, "We could do the compiling of ideas together and assign the writing parts later."

Gary remembered their saying this morning that there was not time to do independent research. He said, "Compile is one thing. New research is another. You are correct in using the term 'compile.'"

# CHAPTER THREE

Ann concluded that with this conversation they had abandoned the adversarial approach. She liked the abandonment but decided it was not the time to say that had happened. She did say, "What do you think Burner meant by 'survival'?"

"I think Burner meant by "survival" to include the things to be done so the animals, the plants, and man could continue to live together in good health and reasonable comfort as we have done in the past. This refers to the physical matters which are necessary to furnish food, shelter, clothing, and space in which to live compatibly with other humans on the planet, with the plants, and with the animals."

Ann quickly added "You know Burner better than I do. I think you have said what Burner would say if we asked him that question. I suspect he would expand and say a lot more things, but whatever he said would be consistent with the definition you have just given. Let us follow that definition until we see that it does not fit the facts."

Gary did not respond immediately. Before he had a chance to say anything else, Ann asked, "What do you think Burner meant by 'prosperity'?"

"I would guess if Burner intended the term 'survival' to apply to the care and use of the physical matters on the earth, he meant the term 'prosperity' to refer to the ability to obtain those physical matters. This would include the energy and efforts of man so that everyone would have enough food, shelter, etc., to satisfy a little more than their personal needs and desires while they live in peace and comfort, and to produce enough savings to create the capital needed to create tools to produce even more and to employ even more people."

"Yes, prosperity is the ability of man to produce more than he needs to barely survive. The extra production can be used to support those who do research, teaching, produce other things—such as the arts and literature and the things that make life more interesting and worthwhile-and to support those who, for some reason, are unable or unwilling to support themselves."

"Yes, that sounds reasonable."

"I am sure, Gary, that survival is broader than just the air, the plants, the water, and the animals. To have survival there has to be activity by the human race. The problem we are to discuss is what has been done by the human race to make the best use of the plants, the animals, the water, and the space to take care of all of the living creatures, including man."

"That sounds very profound. This is going to take time, effort, imagination, and resources. Affecting survival without using or destroying more of the resources than will permit survival is the economic problem of prosperity."

Ann was interested in getting started on the project. She asked Gary, "What is necessary for the survival of the planet?"

"If we believe everything we read and hear, or can imagine, the world is in sad shape right now. It is safe to assume the world is going to get worse unless there are drastic steps taken to protect the animals, the plants, the air, the water, and the space. I believe those statements are correct. I think they are based upon good research."

Gary paused and then said, "Most people who have thought and studied about this have reached many different conclusions, one of which is that the earth is getting overcrowded by people. No one has said the earth is being overcrowded by either plants or animals. More people require more space for human activities. I have overcrowding by people on my list already as a factor of survival."

"That is strange. I have overcrowding by people on my list of factors affecting prosperity."

"I think that means that we both regard overcrowding of people as an important matter in our discussion and article. Since we agree that overcrowding of the planet is an important factor, let's start our discussion there."

Ann liked the fact that Gary had made a specific suggestion. She said, "It seems apparent that in the countries of the world which are at the lowest level of economic advancement and prosperity, there is substantial overcrowding. The economy and the resources, combined with the education level in those countries, keep those countries from even feeding their population with adequate nourishment. Children die. Adults' health is damaged by malnutrition, and they starve, too."

"Overpopulation is involved in both survival and prosperity. If we believe the forecasts, and I am inclined to do so, the situation of overcrowding is getting worse every day. We know there will be more people. We know more space will be needed for those new people in the future. I even believe this future overcrowding is not far away."

"Gary, do you realize what you have said? You have said there are, or soon will be, too many people on this planet. You have not said anything about what can be done about the overcrowding. I would think Burner would like us to have some kind of a suggested solution to the problem of overcrowding."

"What are you going to suggest?"

"People cannot be sent to the dog food factories as was done when horses became obsolete because machines did things better and there was an oversupply of horses. There are very likely to be more people born to add to the overcrowding."

Gary tried to be funny. He said, "If we sterilized every other man, that would cut down on births. In time, older people will die off. If there are not as many new ones to replace them, the population of the earth will decrease. I am not sure who would be able, or even want, to decide who the men are who are going to be sterilized. Would you like to make that selection? I am not very funny, am I?"

16

Ann responded, "What you have just suggested is birth control. That is an emotional and, some people think, a religious matter. Some of my friends talk about birth control as if it were the worst kind of evil. I do not like to think about birth control. I do not believe in birth control, but if overcrowding is a factor in the survival of the planet, then birth control is relevant to the solution of the problem of survival of the world, and it should be discussed in our article. I would be uncomfortable writing on birth control."

It amused Gary to think there was any subject that would make Ann uncomfortable, but he did not say that out loud. He was tactful. He said, "I will not mind making that suggestion, but is it realistic? Is birth control enough? Are we sneaking up on the thought that we should also consider abortion as relevant to the survival of the planet?"

Ann exclaimed, "Oh my! That would be a shocker to Burner. That issue is controversial and emotional for people both pro and con. If Burner had wanted an article on birth control or abortion, or both, I believe he would have said so."

"I doubt that he would have been any more specific than he was."

"Gary, I do not believe in abortion. I feel much more strongly opposed to abortion than I do to birth control. Birth control is an act to avoid a child being started. Abortion is the destruction of a child once the child has started and before the child is born."

"Yes, Ann. I have a hard time guessing what Burner wants sometimes. You remember I thought Burner intended this as a joke. I doubt if he intended to raise the issues of birth control and abortion as any part of what I was to solve in thirty days."

Ann said, "If Burner intended this to be a joke, it would serve him right if we made abortion the focus of what he directed. I would think he does not want to raise such a controversial subject right now. Is abortion a factor about which we want to write?"

"Burner runs the paper. If he does not want to publish what we write, it is his responsibility. If birth control and abortion are relevant to fulfilling his direction to write on the survival and prosperity of the planet, we should include a discussion of those two subjects in our conclusion. They should not be the only ideas we cover. All Burner can do is fire us. I have been with him so long I do not think he would fire us. He would just laugh."

"I am opposed to abortion. We could recommend abstinence. Complete abstinence would depopulate the earth in just a few decades. There would be deaths, but no births. We can include abstinence as a factor in the survival of the planet. My guess is that abstinence is not what Burner wants us to discuss either. I doubt if abstinence would work because I doubt if there will be abstinence."

# CHAPTER FOUR

Gary replied to Ann, "You said you are opposed to abortion. How strongly do you feel in your opposition? In other words, do you feel so strongly against abortion that you would picket an abortion clinic to keep ladies from entering to receive their services? Would you support the shooting and killing of doctors who perform abortions?"

"I am not sure. I believe abortion is the killing of defenseless beings. Killing any being is wrong. It is murder. We should not let people get away with killing and murder. Maybe someone will have to take the law into their own hands and stop the killing of innocent beings. Maybe someone will have to commit one crime, such as killing the persons conducting the abortions, in order to prevent another crime as serious as the killing of innocent little beings."

Gary laughed a little at the enthusiasm Ann was putting into her statements. He replied, "We are different. Like you, I do not believe in abortion, but I do not feel so strongly that I would physically prevent someone else from exercising his or her right to have a different opinion or putting that opinion into operation. Everyone has a right to disagree."

"In general I agree with that, too. But killing is such a horrible crime it must be an exception. We cannot let other people have the right to put into operation their own opinions when killing is involved even if the killing is of their own child to be."

"Ann, we are adversaries. I can now see we each have a prejudice and preconceived belief that abortions are wrong. We each have a prejudice and preconceived belief on the rights of other people to have different ideas and to put those beliefs into operation. Our beliefs on the rights of others to have a different opinion are different."

"It looks that way. Should we fight about it?"

"No, but we can analyze our conflicting prejudices. If we have conflicting preconceived ideas, we should look at each conflict with an open mind if we can."

"You know, Gary, each of us was brought up to know it was wrong to have a closed mind on any subject. As journalists we have to have open minds. We have to know we might be wrong. We should discover for ourselves whether we have closed minds before someone else discovers it for us."

"Burner wants us to make an objective analysis. At first it looked as if we thought a factor we should analyze was birth control and abortion. Now I am inclined to believe the first factor we have to analyze is our own prejudices and perhaps the whole subject of prejudice itself."

Ann was quiet for a moment while she gathered her thoughts. Then she said, "Yes, we should tackle prejudice first. I would not want anyone to think I could not have an open mind."

"The matter of prejudice should be included in our article, too."

"I do not think I would have any emotional hang ups in writing something on the subject of prejudice."

"Okay, Ann, how do we start on fighting prejudice? If this is to be included, we should take some notes. Perhaps both of us ought to write down the ideas we reach in our discussion. Then we will be prepared to put something about prejudice into our article."

"I have been making some notes as we talked. I do not think there are any laws which say we cannot be prejudiced and absolutely are required to maintain open minds."

"An open mind may be the essence of an educated person and the basis of progress."

Before Ann could reply, Gary added, "An open mind may also be the most necessary factor in a successful democratic form of government."

"Yes, it is a cinch that in a democracy everyone is not going to agree on everything."

"If we are going to live in peace with each other—which means survive with each other—which also means survival of the world—we have to learn to get along with other people's ideas."

Ann then said, "No one will always be in the majority on everything."

"There is a lot of benefit in protecting the minority and their right to disagree, especially when we happen to be in the minority."

"I am sure, Gary, there will be times when I am in the minority. Right now you and I disagree. There are only two of us, so we are neither the majority nor the minority, but when we bring someone else in, one of us is going to be in the minority."

"If you are in the minority, Ann, don't you want the right to have other people respect your views?"

"You are trying to destroy my prejudice."

Gary said, "Sure, that is what our discussion is all about."

"But minority ideas should not be respected on everything."

"Why not, Ann?"

"A minority that believes in killing their neighbors as a method of solving disputes cannot be tolerated in a civilized society."

"Would such an idea fit the idea of 'might makes right?' We all know, as history shows, might is not always right. We cannot condone the idea of might is right."

"Since, I suppose, I am required to have an open mind, Gary, perhaps I should reconsider my prejudice about the ideas of people who believe the right to an abortion should be respected. Perhaps I should reconsider whether their ideas should even be tolerated. It will be hard, but I will try."

Gary said, "Opposition to abortion is, in part at least, based on what some people think is a religious belief."

"Is there any religious authority for having an open mind and respecting the ideas of others?"

"I believe there is. Isn't the Golden Rule set out in the Bible?"

"I think so. We could check."

"I think I know where it is in the Bible. There is a Bible in my desk drawer. My mother gave it to me when I graduated from college. I brought it here to the office when I was writing an editorial. I have never taken it home. I will go get it."

As Gary got up to go to his office Ann watched him move. He was very graceful. To her he looked kind of nice as he walked away. Ann thought to herself, "What a strange fellow he must be. He pretends to be a big tough newspaper man, yet he believes in ladies first. Now she knew he kept a Bible in his desk. She wondered if any other newspaper men kept Bibles handy. She wondered if Gary had ever used the Bible in any of his writing. She wondered if Gary had ever looked at the Bible at any other time than when he had been writing that editorial. She would try to guess by looking to see if the Bible looked worn in any way when Gary brought it back.

Ann resolved that she wanted to get better acquainted with Gary and his ideas. All of his ideas were a little obscure to her right now.

It was not long before Gary was back with the Bible. As Gary walked towards her Ann notice again how nice he looked.

Ann could not tell from looking at the cover of the Bible if it had ever been used at all.

Gary said, "Here it is. This is one of the places the Golden Rule appears in the Bible. It is in Mark 12:28. It says that Jesus, the son of God, was talking and answering questions. You would agree, Ann, wouldn't you, that Jesus, as the son of God, should be our strongest authority? I know of no way to dispute what Jesus says if you have any Christian feelings at all."

"Yes."

Gary looked down as he read. He said, "In this passage someone asked Jesus, "Which is the first commandment of all?' Jesus answered that the first commandment is to love God with all your heart and all your soul. Then Jesus said that the second commandment is, 'Thou shalt love thy neighbor as thyself.' Then Jesus said, 'There is no other commandment greater than these.'"

It was Ann's turn to speak. "That is the King James Version you are reading. I know there are other versions of the Bible, but I am sure that the other versions say in substance the same thing. I think the Golden Rule was described by Jesus at other times and at other places in the Bible."

"Yes, that statement of Jesus" seems to have been set out in the Bible several times. I do not know whether there are several references to the same statement of Jesus or whether Jesus spoke on the Golden Rule more than once. I would guess he did. We can look at the other verses in the Bible."

"Let's not do that right now."

"No. I see that for our purpose the different verses say about the same thing. The Golden Rule has to be the commandment that all of us should follow first."

"I am beginning to see what you are driving at, Gary. I see how the Golden Rule includes having an open mind and not having prejudice. It means that if I want the freedom to have respect for what I believe, I must treat my neighbor, which means everyone, with the same respect for what he or she believes. You are saying I must give respect to what others believe."

Gary answered, "Having such respect does not mean you and I should change our view and beliefs about abortion being wrong. It only means we should accept the right of others to have their own beliefs on abortion. We can use democratic processes to affect the legal results. We can hope the majority will agree with us."

"Yes, I can now see the Golden Rule means we cannot advocate obstruction at abortion clinics or tolerate killing of doctors who perform abortions or any intolerance of those who believe differently than we believe."

"I am inclined to accept the word of God as stated by Jesus."

Ann confessed, "I am willing to admit I might be wrong. I do not want to admit I am wrong. It seems the word of God, as stated by Jesus, means we should consider the possibility that others are right and we are wrong."

"You say you can now respect other people's ideas. Respecting other people's views is the essence of an open mind. Do you now respect other people's opinions enough so that you would think a lady, with her doctor's advice, should be permitted to make her own decision to have an abortion of her own child, or not to have an abortion?"

Ann answered, "I pride myself on being unprejudiced. I suppose if I respect other people's right to have their own ideas on other things, I should respect such rights on abortion, too."

Gary waited for Ann to complete what she had started to say. Ann said, "You have convinced me I should give up my prejudice against other persons having a different view than I have about abortion. That does not mean I am going to give up my beliefs against abortion itself."

Gary thought Ann was having a hard time saying what she had just said. He waited until she thought some more. She said, "I am sorry, but I will have to admit to you I must be prejudiced against abortion. I do not think it is right to kill. I do not think anyone should have a right to kill even their own unborn child."

"How are we going to be able to write an objective analysis if we start out prejudiced?"

Ann did not answer, but she did reply with, "I should ask you the same questions to find out if you are prejudiced, too."

"I believe, just as you do now, that I should let people have different ideas than I have. However, when it comes down to abortion and killing, I do not feel the same. I guess I have an open mind on letting people have other ideas than I have, but I, too, am prejudiced against the idea of abortion."

Ann asked, "Are we unable to write the objective analysis on abortion we think Burner wants?" Ann paused as if to think of something new. Then she said, "Maybe we have accomplished something. This is a good time to stop this chatting and to write down what we have been saying about our new conclusions. I want to write my ideas before I start discussing something different. If you do not mind, I will go back to my desk and write this on my computer word processor."

Gary did not want to say he did mind. He was enjoying this time and method of arriving at new ideas. He was reluctant to have the time with Ann interrupted. Nevertheless, he said, "I think I will go to my desk and write my version of these ideas, too. We can compare them in the morning."

"No, we can compare them right after noon tomorrow. I still have to finish what I was doing when you asked me about the Burner memo. I have some errands to do I had scheduled for after work today before we decided to work on our regular things each morning and on this project in the afternoon. So I will have to go soon."

Now it was Gary's turn to watch Ann as she arose from the desk and walked away out of the office. He did not get any new ideas from what he was seeing which had not occurred to him before. Nothing was disappointing to him.

Gary went to his own office and desk. He put paper into his old manual typewriter. He started typing about the things they had just discussed.

The next time Gary looked up from his typewriter, it was past quitting time. All of the employees working in the area outside Gary's office were gone. Ann was gone, too.

# CHAPTER FIVE

Ann did get to the room where she and Gary were working before Gary returned from lunch. She was proofreading what she had written when Gary walked in and sat down. Ann spoke first.

"As I was writing, it occurred to me that what we talked over and the conclusions I think we reached yesterday on respecting the ideas of others apply not only to the matter of prejudice on abortion, but to all kinds of prejudice."

"What do you mean, Ann?"

"Well, maybe it is not a part of the subject of what Burner asked us to do, but you know and I know there is a great deal of prejudice in this country about race and the color of a person's skin. I always have thought I had an open mind and did not have racial prejudice. I still do not think I have racial prejudice. When we were talking yesterday, I could see the Golden Rule applies to racial prejudice, too."

Gary replied, "I suppose it does. However, prejudice about racial matters is not prejudice against the ideas of other people. It is prejudice against the color of the skin only, not against ideas."

"Well, that may be true, but prejudice itself is covered by the Golden Rule. Maybe the Golden Rule applies to racism more than it does to differing ideas on abortion."

"Let's think about that a bit. Let us see how our thoughts come out."

Ann said, "Yes, everyone has some control over his thoughts and ideas, but no one has control over the color of his or her skin. No one can choose his or her parents. People have the same color of skin as their parents. I did not chose my parents. I have the same color of skin that they do. Well, not exactly. My father spends a lot of time outdoors, so his face and arms are a rougher color. I spend so much time indoors that my skin is different, but you know what I mean."

"Right. I did not select my parents either. You are saying that since the color of one's skin is not under anyone's control there should be no racial prejudice because the color of the skin is different. Yes, I see what you are saying. The Golden Rule means we should treat our neighbors, which means everyone, as ourselves. We are all alike. None of us selected our parents or the color of our skin."

Ann responded, "You've got my idea. I wonder why I never thought of the racial situation and prejudices in this way before?"

"Neither have I."

Ann continued with her thoughts, "Then after that thought occurred to me, I thought about other prejudices that exist today. You mentioned one of them a little yesterday when you told me of your ideas on 'ladies first.' You know there is gender prejudice. Some people think men are better than women. There is talk about what is women's work. There is talk that a woman's place is in the home. I think I have even heard it said that a man should keep his wife barefoot and pregnant."

"You have never heard me say any of those things."

"Oh, I am sorry. I did not mean to say you have such ideas. I was just saying such ideas exist, or used to exist, in this country. I know those ideas exist much more strongly in some of the European countries and in families which have not been away from European ways very long."

"Do not ignore the Arabian countries nor the Oriental countries. They have different standards between men and women than exist in the United States. I would think the most equality between genders is here in the United States. I will agree that a little of the prejudice that the genders are different still exists here."

"I am a woman. I was born a girl. I did not have any choice as to whether I was to be a boy or a girl. When I was little I must have been a tomboy or something. I remember I wanted to be a boy. I told that to my father one day. He said God made me a girl. He said I should be proud of being a girl."

"I am glad you were born as a girl."

"Don't confuse me. This is a serious business discussion. My point is that people do not have a chance to choose the gender they will be and, therefore, the gender they will stay for the rest of their lives."

"You are now about to tell me that because no one has such a choice, there should be no prejudice about which gender one is."

Ann said, "Right. The Golden Rule applies to such prejudice, too."

"You have interesting thoughts. They are correct, but are they relevant to what we must write for Burner?"

"Do not mislead me. I have not finished telling you what else occurred to me while I was writing about prejudice regarding abortion."

"Let me see if I can guess."

"That will be interesting , too, if you can. Go ahead and try."

Gary then said, "You have said the Golden Rule, when applied, should eliminate prejudice on matters upon which no one has any control. You mentioned racial prejudice. You mentioned gender prejudice. Another matter upon which Congress has enacted laws to protect people from prejudice is prejudice because of age. No one has the privilege of selecting the date of his or her birth. No one has control over his or her own age."

"How did you guess that was what I was thinking?"

"Is my guess what you were about to say?"

"Yes. I did not know my ideas were expressed so clearly."

"So, Ann, you did not think I was smart enough to see the next step in your reasoning?"

"No, I am sorry if you got such an idea. I am just amazed at how much you and I seem to think alike."

"It is fun, too."

"This is a business office, and this is a business matter. Do not tease me. I have something else to say."

"I am not surprised, Ann. Go ahead. I will not try to guess this time."

"I have not thought about whether these ideas on prejudice against race, gender, and age are a part of the subject that Burner assigned to us. Last night a little poem came to me about this. I do not think we should put the poem in the article."

"I did not know you were a poet, Ann."

"Oh, I used to write poetry for fun. I put some in a couple of articles I wrote here at the paper, but before I turned the articles in I took the poetry out. Sometimes poetry can express an idea in less words and with more feeling."

"Yes, I have noticed that a few times. If it is not too long, maybe we can fit it in some place. Do you have it with you?"

"Of course. You did not think I would mention the subject of the poem unless I liked the poem and had it with me, did you?"

"No. Do not keep me in suspense. Read me the poem."

"I am not sure I like the last two lines."

"Let me see what I think of it."

"Okay. I will read it.

Our Parents None Of Us Did Choose.
Their Color We Will Never Lose.
Our Gender None Of Us Did Pick.
With Our Gender We All Must Stick.
Our Birth Date We Did Not Select.
Our Age We Do Have To Accept.
We Are All Exactly The Same
We All Stay Just The Way We Came."

"I like it. You are correct. Everyone comes with the color of their parents, the gender they had when they were born, and the age that comes from the date they were born. No one has any choice on these. No one can change any of these things. Therefore, we are all alike. There is no way anyone can be different from the way we were born. We must stay the way we are sent into this world by God. Those are good thoughts. They were well expressed in the poem. The poem is a nice quick way of summarizing the whole situation of prejudice. What is wrong with the last two lines?"

"They just do not feel right."

"The lines all rhyme. Each line has the same number of syllables. They say what you wanted to say. They have a nice ring in the poem. I suppose the last two lines could be left off, or they could be changed. If we can fit the poem into the article, let's do so. I think we can fit it in. First we have to know what else is to be in the article."

Gary was quiet for some time. Ann did not interrupt him. Finally Gary said, "As I think some more about racial prejudice, it occurs to me that the problem of racial prejudice may be more destructive to the survival and prosperity of the world right now than is prejudice against abortion. The problem of abortion is to save the earth from overcrowding, which is near but is not yet fatal to the way most of us live today. But racial prejudice is destroying harmony and damaging the way we live today."

"Gary, I do not understand what you mean."

"People of color, or some of them at least, seem to feel that they are treated as second class citizens. They think that they do not get as good jobs and do not get as good pay in the jobs they do get. Some feel that they do not get the same treatment by government as others do. They feel that the police pick on them just because of their color. They feel that the schools do not give them the same quality of education as schools give to others. They resent this treatment and are demanding equality more and more. They are very impatient for better treatment."

"I know about that feeling, but how does that affect survival and prosperity?"

"If people of color do not receive as good an education and as good jobs and as good pay as others, they are not able to produce as much as others and may, in fact, become dependent upon government. Those who work and receive smaller pay will not be able to produce as much toward total prosperity, education, research, the arts, and assistance of those who are unable to care for themselves. They will not be able to produce savings which will provide the capital which is needed to increase production facilities and to create wealth. There is less total prosperity because of the discrimination which results from racial prejudice."

"Gary, there are government programs and laws to prevent this discrimination."

"These laws may not be enough. They divert efforts to produce prosperity. When the laws are enforced by programs which are sometimes called 'affirmative action' this means that there is new discrimination based on the color of the skin."

"But Gary, these affirmative action programs are needed not only to help make up for past discriminations, but to reduce discrimination now."

"I am not arguing against these programs. I am just saying that when any action is taken on the basis that there is a difference in color, such action emphasizes the differences instead of eliminating the differences. It seems to me that the answer to the problem of prejudice over the difference in the color of a person's skin should be to eliminate treatment based upon the color of the skin and to treat all people alike regardless of their color. Different treatment should only result when people are different in some significant way. The color of a person's skin is not a significant difference. The color, as we discussed earlier, results from a person being born with the same color of skin that his parents had. If there is no other difference, then there should be no other treatment than to treat everyone alike. People should be judged on their own merits and what they can produce for themselves and their families. Giving some preference to one of color for a good reason is just as bad as giving some preference to one who is not of color for a bad reason. In fact, it is worse. It gives official recognition to what may be an assumed fact-that is that the people of color are different and need help. The conclusion is inescapable that those who think the people of color need help also think that the people of color are inferior."

"Gary, I do not believe that anyone is inferior because of their color."

"I do not either. But that has to be the basis of helping people of one color more than helping the people of another color. That is what I am saying. I think the practice of different treatment, whether it is called discrimination or reverse discrimination, is wrong. I believe that such treatment is counterproductive. I believe that equal treatment for everyone should be the goal."

"Gary, I do not agree although what you have just said does make some sense. I agree that efforts to eliminate this prejudice and eliminate different treatment is needed. I do agree that this prejudice and different treatment of people who are actually alike except for the color of their skin does affect prosperity, and, therefore, affects survival. I agree that the subject should be mentioned in our article, but I do not think that we have the solution, and I do not think we should advocate abolition of affirmative action programs and other efforts to give equal treatment to persons of all colors."

"Well, that may be as far as we can go in the time we have to get our article written. We started off recognizing that we would not be able to give solutions and answers to all the world's problems that will affect survival and prosperity."

"Sometimes analyzing the problem suggests its own answer. Our saying that this prejudice damages the survival and prosperity of us all can be interpreted as our saying that great effort must me made by everyone to eliminate this prejudice. Everyone should be treated alike. Can you agree with that?"

"Of course. We cannot treat everyone alike by treating some differently."

# CHAPTER SIX

When they met again Ann spoke first. "My writing style might be different enough from yours that it would appear the authors of the parts were different people. We will have that problem anyhow. After the first draft we can smooth it up together."

"That is a good suggestion."

"There is more to discuss and to include on the subject of the survival of the world than birth prevention and prejudice. There are things to do with cleaning up the air, the water, the garbage, etc., which we will want to include. It may be we will not be able to offer different solutions from those that have already been made by others."

"It is not likely that we will have new ideas on every part of the problem of the survival of the earth and its prosperity."

Ann said, "I think we have just made a good start on a plan in writing this article. I like to put some 'bang' into everything I write. Can we have something new and not just redo the same subjects other writers have already covered many times?"

"Before we decide, Ann, that birth prevention and prejudice are factors of survival and prosperity which we want to discuss, perhaps we should consider some other things, too. Perhaps we should list the items on prosperity that are important factors."

"Yes, Gary, prosperity, we have decided, is when the total human race can produce more than it consumes. When that happens there would be time and resources which could be dedicated to supporting learning, recreation, creating things of beauty, and comfort. With such prosperity, each person would be able to furnish an education to his or her children. More research and proper education would create the ability and the knowledge to produce even more. With prosperity, care could then also be given to those who are not able to produce for themselves."

"You are saying this better than I can say the same thing."

"Research, which requires time away from producing for that day's needs, could show us how to produce even more. Agricultural research would demonstrate how to produce more food, which would reduce or eliminate the danger of overpopulation."

There were many other things which they discussed. Ann and Gary considered the advances yet to come in science, which could create even more prosperity. They did conclude there were no more lands in which to physically expand on this planet. They thought about what could be done in space. They recognized that man was already working on using wide areas of the universe for the production of food and the expansion of areas needed by man.

"Gary, Burner asked us to discuss the survival and prosperity of the planet. If the form of government and law is relevant to how many children are born, are we to include in our analysis conclusions about government, too?"

"The type and cost of government affects how much prosperity there may be."

"Yes. Without freedom of speech and action, people will not be able to cure their problems."

"Government is involved in all the factors influencing prosperity."

"There are countries, Gary, which are democracies in fact as well as in form, where the population is predominately of the Catholic faith. In those countries all forms of birth prevention except abstinence are discouraged, as I understand it. I think we ought to avoid trying to analyze those countries policies and tactics."

"Opposition to abortion is a matter we will not be able to ignore, Ann, no matter where it occurs."

"There are places in the United States where there are more people than local government seems to be able to accommodate, while keeping the air clean and not damaging the environment."

Gary sat quietly, waiting for Ann to complete her observation, and then replied, "Other aspects of the survival of the earth and of prosperity must be included in our article, too."

# CHAPTER SEVEN

They then turned their thoughts to things other than birth prevention and the environment as factors in survival and prosperity.

Strangely, as Ann and Gary discussed these other factors, they did not find much disagreement between themselves. A lot of the aspects they discussed had not been considered by either of them before. There was a lot of debate between them. They came to conclusions which they could endorse and could include in their article.

They concluded that the abortion debates and the birth prevention activities were disturbing to many people. These disputes themselves were disruptive to the ability of people to create prosperity.

They could see education was essential to being productive.

The cost of government, they concluded, was counterproductive.

Taxes which were levied for some purposes other than raising revenue, such as those designed to soak those who could produce things and which favored the persons with a vote who did not pay taxes anyhow, were not productive to prosperity. Such taxes were counterproductive. Those kinds of taxes discouraged production.

There were lots of problems in the world which affected prosperity and, therefore, survival.

The more they discussed and thought, the more they concluded that activity which did not result in production was something to be discouraged. Nonproductive activity interfered with prosperity.

Gary said, "Crime is predatory and not productive. It is worth a great effort and expense to fight crime. In the time we have for this article, we will not be able to set out complete answers for the elimination of crime."

"Crime is the result of someone not being able or willing to produce enough for his own needs or desires, plus being greedy. Greater prosperity is probably the answer to crime."

Gary followed this line of thinking by saying, "Gambling produces nothing. In some places some sorts of gambling are a crime in this country. For a long time all kinds of gambling were considered a crime. Then the representatives of the people who make the laws started making exceptions. Some kinds of gambling were made legal under regulated circumstances. The gambling promoters discovered that the government and the people could be legally bribed with their own money.

"All that is necessary to get approval for certain forms of gambling is to cut the government in on a very small portion of the proceeds. Maybe the proceeds should be called 'loot.' Gambling has been permitted under some restrictions, one of which is a license and taxes on the amount wagered."

"Yes, Gary, historically government has protected the public from gambling because it was not a productive activity. Gambling spawned financial ruin for people who could not regulate themselves. Gambling created other evils." Ann was quiet for a minute while she thought through what she had just stated. Then she said, "The gambling promoters encouraged government to have a conflict of interest. In order to get a small portion of the wagers made in gambling, some states abandoned their thought of the protection of their citizens, succumbed to the bribe, violated their duty by creating a conflict of interest, and capitulated in order to get a very small portion of the money gambled."

"Yes, gambling is a deterrent to prosperity. We can put that in our writing, too."

Gary then said, "Taxes are a burden on productivity and, therefore, on prosperity. Taxes pay for the cost of government. Some kinds of taxes deter prosperity. The burdens of government hurt or slow prosperity." Gary discussed a new idea to him. "If lack of prosperity is one of the causes of crime, then since government and taxes slow and interfere with prosperity, it follows that government itself is one of the causes of crime."

The two of them were letting their ideas race after each other. Ann said, "The cost of health care slows prosperity."

"Health care is so expensive that many people cannot afford the care. Public welfare then furnishes the care from funds obtained from taxes, which could be used for something else either by the government or by the people who pay the taxes. That slows prosperity."

Gary and Ann concluded that democratic government with freedom of speech, which is necessary to democratic government, brings the greatest ability of people to do things for themselves and, therefore, creates the greatest prosperity.

Good universal education for everyone brought great prosperity. Good education was necessary for democratic government to survive. They said that several times but decided that education was so important that mention of education needed to be made several times.

Gary said, "We have an imperfect government. No government is perfect. Democratic governments come a lot closer to perfection than other forms of governing because there are so many people watching their representatives. Freedom of speech makes government officials and employees careful. Government officials and employees can be removed if they do not satisfy their constituents."

Ann added, "Of course, elections are not perfect either, but no one has found a better way to watch over and change government officials, employees, and policies."

"Ann, no matter what part of the world we consider, it is probable that prosperity depends upon the ability of the individuals, as a whole, to provide enough assets to feed and clothe each family and produce a little more."

"Yes. It is probable that no matter what part of the world we consider the key to increasing the production of each individual is in education. We keep coming back to the importance of education to both the survival and the prosperity of the world."

"I have not been taught, maybe I should say 'been educated,' to think in planetary terms. In this day of fast communication and easy travel to almost everywhere, it may be that the rest of the world is like the United States, and the United States is like the rest of the world in the things that we are discussing. It may be that we cannot and should not think in terms of just the United States and not consider the rest of the world."

Ann responded, "A slogan we could modify to fit what we are saying might be 'What is good for the world is good for the United States and vice versa.'"

"Charley Wilson would roll over in his grave if he knew how his remarks about his employer would be treated and mistreated. You have said it very well."

Gary opened the discussion again. "We have wandered about a bit as we discussed what should be in this article. If someone listened to our conversations, they would consider them to be a lot of repetition and uncoordinated thoughts."

"That is all right with me. It has helped me think through these things. When I was in doubt, I could go back and think of a new excuse to come to the same conclusion."

"We can clear up the repetition in our rewrite. I think it is easier to get our ideas on paper first and then to write the final conclusion in proper order.

"How much of this type of discussion should we put in our final article?" Ann asked.

"Our answers could become too long. If we make our article too long, not even Burner will read it. We should not be guided by how long Burner's attention span may be or how busy he is. We should do a good job of covering the subject assigned. We should do a complete and careful analysis and use whatever space is necessary to do that. On the other hand, Burner may not be very different from the readers of this newspaper. What we write is valueless if it is not read."

Ann added, "Yes, it might be dangerous to our own personal prosperity if things in this paper are not read. The paper might go broke. We need to cater to our readers. The slogan probably is 'What is good for this paper is good for us and 'vice versa.'"

"We should not let our self-interest and the self-interest of the paper influence what we include in the article."

"If our article is too long, Burner may delete some of our ideas. On the other hand, Burner may divide the article into sections and run parts on successive days or weeks. TV does that in many mini-series now being produced and shown. If it is too long for one night's program, they just run it several nights. Burner is pretty sharp. That is what he may do. That is what he may have had in mind when he asked me to do this study."

"I hope he does something like that. Otherwise it may turn out to be more like a book than a newspaper article."

"I am glad, Ann, we discussed this. I am now inclined to think we should say the United States and the rest of the world are in the same boat, which is in danger of capsizing."

"I reluctantly agree we should make our article as short as possible and still cover the subject. For myself I am thinking more clearly now. Thank you for educating me. Besides that, it has been fun discussing this with you."

"You have a good imagination, Ann. We have a good outline of a direction to go. I suggest we work separately on these matters for the rest of this afternoon. We can then check with each other in the morning to see what we have done."

Ann nodded agreement and said, "I will go back to my desk. I will not be able to concentrate while being in the same room with you and knowing you are writing about birth prevention, including abortion."

Ann also knew by now that if Gary was sitting across the desk from her, he would be a distraction.

"You are correct. We can get this done faster this way and perhaps better, too."

Ann got up to go. Without any plan or intention, they collided at the door just as they had when they came the first afternoon. This time it was ladies first again. Gary backed away. He let Ann through the door first. This afternoon had been all business.

# CHAPTER EIGHT

Thursday at one o'clock also came with Ann and Gary approaching the same door at the same time. The Bible was still on the desk where they had left it. This time Ann carried a bundle of computer printouts. Gary had some rough draft pages.

Gary sat down first. He watched Ann as she turned, sat down, and pulled herself up to the desk.

"Ann, how did it go?"

"Gary, it is exciting to work on a project with as few directions as Burner gave to us. It is fun to use your own imagination.

"I agree that it is established by most writers that many of the problems of the environment are caused by too many people consuming too many of the resources, including the air and the water. Most writers have concluded that we are approaching the limit of the capacity of the earth to cope.

"But I think there are some things that can still be done before the situation becomes desperate. The total food production capacity of the earth has not yet been reached. In fact, there has been overproduction of food in the United States for many years. Research and imagination will find a way to produce more food for the human race. The earth may be producing more food than is needed at this time. There are places where this food does not get delivered and used. There are people who are hungry in this country. Hunger is caused by political and governmental forces in nondemocratic nations, accompanied by greed and other factors in this country."

Gary started to interrupt and add something but decided that as long as Ann was wound up this tight, it was time for him to keep quiet.

Ann went on. "Hunger caused by nondemocratic governments is not the fault of the environment. That hunger is the fault of preventing the natural economic forces from working. Antitrust laws and democratic government might be the answer to this poor distribution of the food among the people of those nations where people are starving."

"I am not sure, Ann, we will have time to go into these matters of military

34

dictatorships and government by hoodlums. These matters do affect both the survival and the prosperity of the people as a whole although it would seem they are used to create prosperity for a few."

"Gary, what Burner asked us to do covers not only the environment and economics, but politics as well, which comes down to a need for democratic governments over the whole earth."

"There are too many governments which are not responsive to the needs of their own citizens. Is such a situation desperate for the whole planet? It is desperate for the people involved. Some people try to leave their own countries because of this. Other countries do not want to accept them. Immigration and restrictions on immigration will have an effect on the prosperity of the receiving nations."

"I am not ready, Gary, to recommend that our nation alone try to solve the political situations elsewhere in order to help the world survive. I might make that recommendation if I had a chance to study this subject more, but I am not ready to do this in the next twenty-five days."

"We had thirty days, but I wasted three days over the weekend by thinking this was a joke. I think we cannot include the subject of the political situation even though it does seem important to the survival and prosperity of the planet."

"Gary, there are places where the situation is desperate. There is only so much land on the planet. Destruction of the forests can be helped by replanting, but replanting does not create more space. Perhaps there is enough food, but just looking at the space situation may require immediate action in slowing up the expansion of the human race."

"Now, Ann, you have brought the discussion back to birth prevention. I have not arrived at any new conclusions. I observe that in the abstract it is easy to say that birth prevention would affect the size and growth of the world's population in time."

"I recall, Gary, that I learned in college about the theories of Robert Malthus, an English economist. He wrote over one hundred fifty years ago about the problem he foresaw that the world's population would outgrow the food supply. If I recall, Malthus was not completely wrong in his conclusions. He did not take into consideration the great expansion in food production which resulted from research and better methods of food production. He also did not consider that there would be exploration and new parts of the earth dedicated to food production."

"Yes, Ann, I remember that discussion in college, too. Perhaps Malthus was right although ahead of his time. Now the world seems to have been pretty well explored. But even if there are new areas to develop for food production, developing new areas in which to produce food is only postponing the problem, not solving it."

Ann added, "Even space exploration and production of food in space has not been exhausted."

"Perhaps overcrowding is not yet the problem some people envision. However, if something is not done, the problem will arrive sooner or later."

It was Gary who asked, "We keep coming back to birth prevention as a necessary element of both survival and prosperity. Why is it that some people say they are opposed to abortion and birth prevention?"

They both paused.

It was Ann who spoke first. "I was taught abortion was wrong at home and in my church. I never questioned what I was taught. I have not thought about the reasons one way or the other. I was satisfied with that position."

"That is what happened to me, too."

"You know there are many people in the United States who do not have our opinion. Why do they have a different idea than we?"

"I have not objectively analyzed my reasons. Do you suppose, Ann, those who believe in abortion on demand, or variations of that, have objectively analyzed their beliefs any more than we have?"

"There sure has been a lot of dissention and unrest over the subject. The discussion has always been, as I see it, an emotional or a religious discussion."

Gary added, "Soil conservation and environmental protection have been the subject of much thinking and writing. I would say those subjects have been objectively analyzed. All other aspects of survival of the earth have been thoroughly studied."

"Yes, I would say that, too."

"The matters on prosperity that we mentioned, Ann, have all been the subjects of a lot of writing and study. I could not say there is any factor that has not been objectively analyzed. We will have to include these matters in our article. I do not believe, based upon what we have said so far, that we are in disagreement over these items of prosperity. We can start writing on these now."

Ann then said, "Even though my natural inclinations are not to analyze birth prevention, it seems to be a significant factor which we have not objectively analyzed for ourselves, at least."

"When it comes to being specific, as I like to do when I write something, writing about birth prevention will not be easy." Again Gary paused. Ann did not interrupt. Gary went on. "Now, I will try to see the situation logically. I can see that logically birth prevention may be necessary. I still have difficulty in overcoming my emotions. It is against the ethics that I had when I started out in life to be in favor of abortion."

Ann felt sorry for Gary. She felt sympathetic for her own ideas at the same time. She joined Gary's discussion by saying, "I am proud of you for admitting that you are not a big, tough, unemotional, and logical man. I, too, had some of those same feelings. I did not know how to say what you have just said. We must be more alike than I thought. If you feel this way and I feel this way, we will not be able to do this article."

"What can we do? I do not see how we can abandon this idea now. Logically, it is a necessary conclusion."

"No, Gary, we are not going to run away from logic and reality. Logic and reality say there has to be something done about the overcrowding and prospective overcrowding of this planet. What are we going to do?"

Gary said, "Thanks for understanding me and for your sympathy. I have decided that before I can write about any of this, I must confront for myself issues such as legal, moral, and religious ideas, and the question what God's will is. I want to do some thinking, soul searching, so to speak, and maybe do a little research. I think I should talk to some people who know more about the Bible than I do. The teachings of my church may or may not contradict logic. I just do not know. It will take me longer to write about this than I at first anticipated. I have not accomplished anything yet."

Ann, realizing Gary's situation and also realizing it was her attitude on birth prevention, too, said, "We are limited in time. Since the matter of birth prevention will probably be the most difficult part to write, why don't we skip it now. We can go on to the rest first. Then we can come back to birth prevention."

"No," replied Gary. "It cannot be avoided. Perhaps I can continue to think about it while we go on to something else at the same time."

Ann responded, "We are under a time restriction. We cannot do this in the leisure of reflection we want. I believe sometimes things work out better under pressure. Let's go ahead. What is your next idea Gary?"

"Ann, you are not going to like what I am about to say, but no insult is intended. While I was confused and trying to figure out an answer to the problem of overpopulation, it occurred to me that part of the problem is women."

"How can women be responsible?"

"It is not necessarily just women. Women are the ones who bear the children. Women may be, therefore, in the position of being able to do something about the problem. Either men place women in a position where they bear more children than each woman should have, considering her health and financial resources and the resources of the world, or women put themselves in such position."

"Or they do it together."

"My guess is that women permit men to put them in an inferior position. The unsuccessful men, in some parts of the world, just dominate and control the women in their families. They treat their own women worse than a farmer would treat his livestock."

"I have heard that said."

"I can only speculate as to why men would want more children than they can afford or than the world can support. They must hold the children, as well as the women, in low esteem. I have read that a poor man needs more children to work to help support his family. Children may be an economic advantage. A poor man does not have a retirement program or health insurance, so he needs lots of children to take care of him and the family in his old age or in the event of illness."

"No, Gary. With the welfare system in the United States, the children do not have to support their parents in their old age or illness. Gary, has anyone ever done research on the motives of people for having large families?"

"Probably but none that I have seen. I do not know about everything that has been written or all of the research which may have been done. There are so many people, there are probably a lot of explanations of why there are big families. My guess is the men who have larger families than they can support do not think about the consequences when they beget."

"If your guess is correct, how can anything be done about large families?"

"Educated women appear to have fewer children than uneducated ladies. Somehow educated ladies so control the situation that they do not bear more children than the family can raise and educate. Better education for women might be part of the answer to the world's population problem. A change in the status of women, both in their attitude towards themselves and in men's attitudes towards women, might be enough to answer the problem. Do not ask me how. I do not know."

"A change in the status of women to reduce the world's population is a good idea, Gary. I can think such an idea through. I can write those ideas into our article. I will do that while you are struggling with the subject of birth prevention."

"Ann, there is one other subject you might consider including. Since women have the children, and men cannot physically have the children, should men be permitted to vote on matters that affect women only, such as abortion? Is there a rational theory that it is unconstitutional for men, who cannot be affected, to have the right to vote on whether women, who are affected, shall have the right to have abortions? Is that equal protection under the laws?"

Ann laughed and said, "That is a new idea for me. I have read a lot in the last few years. I have not heard such an idea expressed. It might be something new we could include. I can think about that and write it up without any emotional troubles such as birth prevention will give me. In fact, as a woman, I kind of think that way without having studied the legal aspects. Since I might have inborn prejudice on the rights of women, I think you should direct me to write up the situation on the status of women."

"Yes, please do that. We are finding a lot of things to write about, Ann, under Burner's memo. I wonder if Burner thought about how many things are relevant to the subject he selected."

"I will write an objective analysis. No one will be able to tell whether it was written by a man or a woman."

"Ann, there is another thing you can think about concerning laws that regulate or control abortion. There are such laws in this country now. They are being challenged as being unconstitutional. But if we just assume such laws can be enforced, think of the humor in the situation."

"I am not good at seeing humor in anything pertaining to abortion."

"It seems, from what we see now, it is the present minority races and classes that will have the most children if a method of birth prevention is not available. It also seems, from appearances, that it is the same minority groups who favor what they call 'choice' or the legal ability of each women to make her own selection about birth prevention. The minorities may need this choice more than anyone else." Gary continued, "If the minorities are forced by those who insist on what they call 'right to life' to have no 'choice,' the minority groups will probably have more children than they would have had with a choice. In a few years, as minority populations grow, the present minority will not be the minority, but the 'right-to-lifers' will be the minority. They will then be out-voted."

"That would have to be true."

"I would doubt if the 'right-to-lifers' want such a situation. I would think the 'right-to-lifers' are, when they stop to think about it, more interested in preserving the political status quo more or less as it is now. Big families, to be supported on welfare, etc., with the right to vote when the children grow up will change a lot of things."

"They sure will."

"I would guess the 'right-to-lifers' are more interested in avoiding the need to support these big families than they are in forcing children upon those who do not want the children and who will be unable to support them."

Ann said, "I like your humor. I will put that in the article, too. It does not need any research. It is self-apparent."

Both Ann and Gary were quiet for a while. They did not have any more business ready to discuss.

Ann spoke first."I have enough subjects to work on. You need to think without interruptions. I will leave you alone until I am needed."

So saying, Ann, without waiting for a further response, gracefully turned away in the chair, arose, and without a look back, walked out the door to the work area. Gary could not help but notice the manner of the walk. Ann knew Gary was watching. She tried not to exaggerate any movement. Ann realized she was unintentionally throwing signals.

Gary did not understand what was intended, if anything, by the signals. He just sat there watching until she was gone. Habit brought him back to business, which now was this article.

# CHAPTER NINE

Ann did not have any trouble getting down to writing concerning the status of women. Ann found the status of women was a subject which intrigued her. Ann did not need any research. She had read a lot on the matter. She was sure her relevant thoughts would roll out logically one after the other. They did.

Gary, on the other hand, could not get his thoughts going. He realized he had prejudged the situation sufficiently that he knew what final result he would probably reach and would have to reach, but he knew he would have trouble getting there logically.

On the subject of legality of birth prevention measures, Gary decided the office library would not be adequate. On the subjects of morality, ethics, religion, and the will of God, Gary was sure the office library would not produce anything helpful. Gary knew what was in the office library. Gary also was now ashamed his news department library would be silent on the matter of ethics. Perhaps that was one of the problems of the modern news system. There was not enough thought of ethics. No sources were available in the office to help if one wanted to consider ethics.

Gary decided he would go to the college library. There certainly should be materials there that would help him decide, not only what to write, but also what to include. He would not tell anyone at the library what it was he was studying. The librarian might have her own ideas that she would like to have considered. Gary did not want to be influenced right now with others' views.

Gary picked up a pad and some pencils. He put them in an old briefcase. He left the building.

Ann noticed Gary leave. She was not sure how she immediately knew where Gary was going and why. She, too, was ashamed that Gary would not be able to find any help on morality, ethics, and religion in the office library. She felt sad, sympathetic, and proud of Gary all at the same time. She proceeded on with her writing on the status of women.

Walking to the library, about a ten minute stroll, Gary had a chance to think some more. He liked to walk when he was trying to figure out some problem. The telephone never rang when he was walking. Walking in fresh air gave to Gary a mild intoxication and exhilaration which brought on new ideas.

This time the walk, although being outdoors, was not in the fresh air. The presence of the exhaust of the cars, the trucks, and the busses was impressed on Gary's nostrils. The odor gave him ideas. He now knew there had to be an end to such polluting conditions. He felt his errand to the library was somehow directed at putting fresh air in the streets in addition to a lot of other things.

Gary rushed back to the office, trying to get there before closing time. He personally never complied with such time limits. He did not think Ann did either. He wanted to be sure he had another chance to visit with her before she left for the day.

As Gary arrived at the office, he saw that he had been right. He was late. Everyone was gone except Ann. She was still at her desk as if she had not noticed anyone leave. She was busy.

With no one else around, Gary walked to Ann's desk. He pulled up a chair from the desk next to Ann's. He sat astraddle, with the chair back in front of him. He leaned forward on the chair back just as Ann looked up.

"Now, I am more confused than ever," Gary blurted out as Ann took off her glasses. "I spent most of the afternoon at the library. I found that either I do not know how to use the library indexes, although I think I do, or the library does not have many materials on ethics and morality which would help me in writing for people who do not have predetermined ideas. What was there was on religion. The material in the library did not have much detail on the will of God. The material I found was so remote as to be useless to me. Why would I think of a perspective no one else used?"

Before Ann could say anything, Gary continued, "I did find some materials on abortion, but they were mostly matters of political pro or con without much objectivity as far as I could tell."

"Weren't there news summaries of what people had said, either pro or con?"

"Oh, yes, Ann, there was material on news reports about what people who opposed abortion said about taking the law into their own hands to close abortion clinics and to keep women from entering the clinics. There was a lot of that sort of thing. I found nothing profound on why such people should be so convinced and emotional on the subject."

"Gary, I am surprised. I am sure you know how to use the library indexes."

"It may be that writers and researchers are afraid to discuss the matter objectively or to conduct original research."

"That is no surprise."

"I did find, however, some material on what happens in the mother's body imme-diately after conception. These were health-type or sex education-type materials. We probably do not need much medical or scientific information for our article. I may have found enough."

"Gary, I am sure there are people who consider that life begins at conception, whereas others believe life begins at birth. Those two ideas make quite a bit of difference. One could come to different answers depending upon when one con-siders that life begins."

"Oh yes, there is a lot of difference of opinion. There does not seem to be any medical material which discussed conception as the beginning of life instead of birth as the beginning of life." Gary paused, as if to think, or take a breath. Then he said, "I found in scientific and medical circles there is nothing which can be considered as any kind of a human being for quite a while after conception. Now, in legal matters, I found that after the opinion of the Supreme Court of the United States on January 22, 1973, in the case of Roe v. Wade, the legislatures of some states, with varying degrees of promptness, passed statutes on the subject of abortion. I do not think those statutes help very much one way or the other in what we are discussing."

Ann did not say a word or attempt to interrupt as Gary rushed through what he had to say. She did not sit quietly, however. Nor was she internally inactive. Gary's feelings of confusion were contagious. Ann was catching whatever disease Gary had acquired.

When Gary stopped to catch a breath, Ann moved in. She said, "That library must have as much material as any library. If you did not find the materials, they must not exist. If they do not exist, there has not been enough thinking on the subject. If we are confused as to what is right and wrong about this, most people must be utterly indifferent or as confused as we are. What significance did you think you would find in the health-type and sex education discussions?"

"I found from health and sex education books that there actually is such a period of time after conception and before viability."

Ann concluded, "That means, it would seem to me, that the ethical, moral, religious, legal, and health considerations are different for the period before viability than they are for the period after viability. Gary, the fact there is a different situation does not mean it is right to cause an abortion before viability and not right to do so after viability."

"You are correct, Ann. The rule of right and wrong could be the same for both periods. The disagreement on this seems to be where emotional dispute arises."

"Did you say that in Roe v. Wade in 1973, the United States Supreme Court made a decision on abortion legality which is different for the period before viability than for the period after viability."

"I do not remember saying so, but that is my understanding of what happened."

Ann then said, "That was a long time ago. Think how many more people there would now be in the United States to add to the overcrowding here if the decision in Roe v. Wade had not been made. That is long enough ago so there would be some second generation children unborn because their parents were unborn."

"Yes. Think how many more people will be added to the overcrowding in the next few years if the decision in Roe v. Wade is reversed. Ann, even after concluding and convincing myself that there is a great danger to the survival of the world when we have too many people, I am still confused as to what is the correct solution."

Both sat there for a period of time which might be judged of different lengths depending upon whether one was involved in the discussion or merely observing.

Finally, Ann reached over, touched Gary's hand, and said, "I am sorry this is confusing to both of us. I am glad though that both of us are sensitive enough so this does confuse us."

"The reasoning that abortion is all right in the period before viability and not right in the period after viability seems to me to be a little evasive. Is not that just playing with words? After all, whatever had been done to start towards viability had already happened. A life would come as soon as the fetus was old enough, big enough, and strong enough, without any action by any human other than caring for the mother. Anything done after conception to change the situation and stop the child from coming would be killing."

"You are at least partially right. Maybe you are completely right. To reach the conclusion that abortion is killing, one would have to assume life begins at the time of conception. No one would know the instant conception happened. No one would know when viability arrived, either. The parties would know what they had done, but they would not know for some time the effect of what they had done or that they had actually created a life.

"Both the law and medicine apparently take the position that life does not commence at conception. It is confusing, isn't it?"

"Yes, I do not know what position we should take."

"Let us give this subject a rest for a while and think about something else. Maybe it will look different later."

There was a long pause. Then Gary said, "Do you ever eat?"

Ann was surprised. Should she consider such a question as an invitation to dinner as a date or as something else? She replied, "Of course I do. I am hungry. I agree a little pause in our discussion may help us to become less confused."

Gary had not planned this very well. He had not thought about inviting Ann for dinner, but it suddenly had appeared to be a good idea. He said, "May I take you to some place where we can eat and discuss things. I promise not to talk about this article."

"I would be delighted, but you do not have to make such a promise. I am not dressed for anything other than business. I hope you do not mind. Let me freshen up a bit. I will be right back."

So saying, Ann lifted herself to a tall posture, turned, and walked away, sending Gary the same message he had observed earlier when she had left the room. Gary stayed there, astraddle of the chair. After Ann was out of sight, Gary went off to freshen up himself.

# CHAPTER TEN

Ann and Gary went out of the office and down the street to a nearby restaurant which was not fancy and did not serve liquor or have music. No one noticed them. No one eavesdropped on their conversation. It appeared that they were two professional people discussing a serious professional matter while they took a break in a long day, with the full intention of going back to the office. This seemed to be a man-woman date-type situation where each was a little hesitant and reserved with the other.

Gary went on a talking jag, telling Ann about himself, his home, his family, the things he liked to do, the things he wanted to do, and his vague, flexible plans for the future.

Ann was a good listener. She looked interested, as if she wanted to know the meaning of each and every word.

After a while it was Ann who was doing the talking while Gary was a good listener. He was apparently anxious to learn of Ann's home, family, the things she liked to do, what she wanted to do, and her vague plans for the future.

During this dinner (which the waiter thought was taking a very long time) a no-touch rule (if there was one) was broken but only by a quiet pat of Ann on Gary's hand when she was quietly impressed.

Suddenly at the same time, they both noticed the hour of the evening. Their demeanor changed as if to say "I have to work tomorrow." Gary helped Ann with her jacket. He then pulled back Ann's chair.

Two working people are entitled to a little privacy after a hard day's work, so we will not follow Ann and Gary out of the restaurant. We will not discuss whether Gary took Ann home, whether she invited him in, whether he left her at her door, or whether there was anything said other than "I will see you at the office in the morning."

# CHAPTER ELEVEN

The Bible was still on the desk when Ann arrived. Gary was already there.

"We have not discussed all of the subject of abortion. What will we say, Gary, when someone cites the Bible injunction, 'thou shall not kill'?"

"Now we are getting into some real problems. Does the injunction 'thou shall not kill' refer to abortion? Last night after I got home I looked in the Bible to find where that statement occurred and how it fit into the context of the other Bible passages. I found a very interesting situation."

"I am curious as to how you can explain that away."

"Let me try. The direction 'thou shall not kill' appears in the Old Testament in Exodus. Do you remember God spoke to Moses and gave Moses some commandments to deliver to the people?"

"Yes."

"There were several commandments there, such as prohibiting adultery, stealing, bearing false witness, coveting the neighbors house or wife, etc. The passage which reads, 'thou shall not kill' appears in Exodus 20:13."

"That is in the Old Testament you said."

"Yes. If I understand, in the same meeting with Moses God gave Moses other directions to deliver to the people. In Exodus Chapter 21, God discussed several kinds of punishment which should be applied for certain offenses. The punishment for killing someone is death, as set out in Exodus 21:12. It says "He that smiteth a man, so that he die, shall be surely put to death."

"In Exodus 21:13-17 there are punishments set out for other acts. For example, at Exodus 21:15 the punishment set out for striking one's father or mother is death. The same punishment is set out at Exodus 21:17 for cursing one's father or mother.

"In Exodus 21:22, just five verses later, there is the specific mention of the deliberate act of causing a miscarriage of a woman, when her husband complains, with the punishment being only a fine payable to the husband. The punishment designated in that passage for causing an abortion or a miscarriage is different and much less than the punishment for killing or for striking one's parents. So maybe we should conclude that God thought killing and abortion were different things."

"I would like to read that passage."

Gary reached for the Bible.

"This is the King James version, Exodus 21:22. It reads, 'If men strive, and hurt a woman with child, so that her fruit depart from her, and yet no mischief follow: he shall surely be punished, according as the woman's husband will lay upon him; and he shall pay as the judges determine.'"

"I have read the Revised Standard Version of that same passage. I have it here in my notes. It is the same, except that instead of saying 'so that her fruit depart from her,' it says 'so that there is a miscarriage.' That seems to me to be the same thing. I did not look at other translations, but I will. They should all say the same thing."

"Gary, what does the passage mean when it says, 'and yet no mischief follow'?"

"I did not look to see if anyone had interpreted that. I think it means that the mother gets well, so there is no other damage than the loss of the unborn child."

"It sounds that way."

"What does it mean when it says 'according as the women's husband will lay upon him'?"

"I think it means when the husband complains."

"If the lady asks for an abortion of herself is there any penalty?"

"Apparently not."

"I am not sure I interpret that passage on miscarriage in Exodus correctly, but it is apparent from that passage in the Bible that causing a miscarriage was not considered by God as a very serious matter, not nearly as serious as striking or cursing one's parents.

"Ann, there is a rule of interpretation of a sentence or paragraph, etc., which I know is applied in some legal matters that might help us understand that passage. It says that if there is specific mention of one thing, the passage does not include other things not mentioned. Using that same reasoning, it would be easy to conclude that God did not think that causing a miscarriage, which is the same as an abortion, is the killing he had just condemned."

"Gary, why haven't we heard anyone talk about that provision in the Bible?"

"I do not know."

"That is the way it looks to me. The injunction 'thou shall not kill' is placed so close in the Bible to the discussion on deliberate miscarriage that it is part of the same sermon."

Ann did not interrupt before Gary said, "There is another passage in the Old Testament which would indicate that we should not feel sorry for the aborted children who are never born, which is what many people seem to feel is outrageous killing."

"I do not remember any such thing."

"It is in Ecclesiastes 4:2-3."

"Read it to me."

"Yes. It reads, 'Wherefore, I praised the dead which are already dead more than the living which are yet alive. Yea, better is he than both they, which hath not yet been, who hath not seen the evil work that is done under the sun.'"

"I wonder why no one has ever referred to that in discussing abortion. That is in the Old Testament just like the parts of the Bible that the 'right-to-lifers' cite as authority against abortion."

"What is said in the Old Testament could not have been said by Jesus. That was before Jesus was born."

"Yes."

"From what I have learned from people who know a lot more about the Bible than I do, the reference in Exodus 21:22 on miscarriage is the only place in the Bible, Old Testament or New Testament, where it could be remotely assumed that God or Jesus talked about abortion."

"Really?"

"It might be safe and accurate, Ann, to categorically say that Jesus has not spoken on the subject of abortion, and therefore, Jesus has not forbidden abortion."

"That would be a startling statement when compared to what is said in many churches and by many religious people today. Gary, that makes it easier for me to abandon my prejudice against abortion. I believed abortion was evil for so long that even with this reasoning I will have some difficulty in approving abortion."

"No, what we have concluded, if we have concluded that much, is that whether abortion is to be permitted is not a religious issue which is discussed in the Bible. Abortion can still be a political issue. The legislative bodies may still be able to permit or forbid abortion or can regulate abortion."

"That does not mean I want to advocate abortion."

"Even without that reasoning and interpretation of Exodus, it would appear, as a matter of medical and legal fact, that an abortion before viability is not killing."

"I am still listening, and I am still unconvinced."

"That is the significance of the time period between conception and viability that I mentioned. Viability means the time when life begins, when the fetus could survive outside of the womb. Until then there is no life. Until then there is no life to kill. At least, that is part of the reasoning that was used in the opinion of the United States Supreme Court in Roe v. Wade. There is nothing in the Bible which disputes that conclusion."

# CHAPTER TWELVE

"Gary, I have thought more on the subject of birth prevention. I believe there are countries in the world where democracy does not prevail, where the political policy has been to encourage a greater population and the birth of more children. Those countries discourage or prohibit birth prevention measures. I am not sure I know the reason. Perhaps it is to have more population for a larger army or to have cheap labor or whatever the dictator has in mind. Maybe the dictator uses religion as a rationalization. I do not know."

"I do not think we should try to analyze everything, Ann."

"Many of those countries have changed their governments in the last few years. We do not know if the change will change their policy on birth prevention."

"Ann, for a lady who did not want to discuss birth prevention, you have done alot of thinking about it."

"No, Gary, I am not afraid to discuss the problem. I just do not want to discuss the wisdom of the policy of birth prevention or the methods."

"I do not think, Ann, you have finished what you started to say."

"That is correct. I also notice there are countries, at least one, where democracy does not prevail but large families are discouraged, with even criminal penalties for having more than an alloted number of children."

"That is too much government interference."

"Government policy varies with the needs of the country and the nature of the control over or by the people. Where people govern themselves, at least one would think, they would have a better answer."

# CHAPTER THIRTEEN

"It is fun discussing this with you, Ann."

"Now, Gary, do not get personal on company time. I appreciate your thoughts about me. I might have some similar thoughts about you someday. But I suggest we should discuss personal matters on our own time. I suggest we do that at my apartment tonight during dinner. Yes, this is an invitation to you to come to my home to share my dinner. I promise my dinners are good. In fact, I was trying to figure out a good way to bring up the subject of this evening and inviting you, instead of you inviting me. Thanks for giving me the opportunity to invite you."

"Ann, I have told you I was brought up to think 'ladies first.' I also believe that 'ladies first' is not to be followed when it comes to a man and woman in their social life with each other. I was taught that it was the man who was expected to start things. I do not feel abused that you have decided to change this rule for tonight. I am very glad you invited me. In fact, if you will not feel insulted by my saying so, I have been curious about some of your culinary skills. I have wondered how I might tactfully hint I would like to come to your apartment."

"You do not have to hint with me. If you want to come to my apartment, I am happy. Just say so."

"It would not be proper for a man to invite you to his apartment. Besides, I would be ashamed to have you see how I live."

Ann answered, "Times are different now. There is nothing forward or aggressive or significant in a lady inviting a man whose company she enjoys to her apartment for dinner. It is not an invitation for anything else. I assume you realize that."

"Ouch. I deserved that. I did not intend to hint for anything more than you have just said."

Ann stood up. She said, "I invited you to my apartment for dinner tonight. You accepted. This means nothing more for me than that you have accepted."

"This means nothing more to me than you have invited me. I am pleased you did."

"Gary, I am sure you know me well enough by now to know I do not do things without being prepared. My invitation was premeditated. I have done some preparation for the meal. Perhaps you do not know, but a nice meal takes some last minute preparations. So, if you do not mind, I will go home now. I suggest you arrive at about seven o'clock. Gary, do not decide to be gallant and bring something. I have done the preparation. I do not want you to bring anything other than yourself."

"Are you sure I cannot bring anything?"

"No, just yourself. You know where my apartment is."

"I know where the outside of the front door to your apartment is."

Ann looked up. She gave Gary a sly smile. "Well, tonight you may come in."

With that, Ann stood up, walked out of the small office where they had been working, put on her jacket, and left the building.

Gary just sat there with a smile. He said to himself that one should not try to predict what that lady would say, do, or think. She was certainly surprising and also interesting. Gary also said to himself that Ann was pretty and was getting prettier every day. He wondered why. Was she wearing different clothes to make her prettier, or was the change all in Gary? He decided it might be a little of both.

As Ann walked away, Gary watched. He did not like to see her going away although he thought it was a pleasant sight. He preferred to see her coming towards him. As she passed from view, Gary noticed a new feeling of heaviness in his chest. He wondered if it was loneliness.

# CHAPTER FOURTEEN

Gary went to his own apartment, took a shower and put on his best suit, a white shirt, and a red and blue patterned tie. He checked his shoes. He thought they were polished. He looked in the mirror. He decided he looked pretty good.

At exactly 7:00, by Gary's wrist watch, Gary knocked on Ann's apartment door. No sooner than one knock had been made, Ann swung the door wide open, half bowed while she pulled one arm back in a graceful swing, and stood aside as Gary entered the apartment.

"Welcome to my home."

Ann was not dressed as she had been dressed at the office. Now she was wearing a bright red blouse which was not tight but was tight enough to hint at what lay below. The neck line was high upon her neck. She was wearing long red dangling earrings which matched the color of the blouse. She wore no other jewelry, unless it was a wrist watch which Gary could not see. The blouse had long wide sleeves coming down almost to her thumbs. Ann's glasses were nowhere to be seen.

Ann also was wearing black slacks with wide loose bottoms which made the slacks flow, almost as if she were wearing a long wide skirt. Below the slacks there were some graceful red high-heeled shoes. Gary did not remember Ann wearing such high heels before. The blouse, the earrings, Ann's fingernail polish, her lipstick, and the shoes were all the same shade of red.

Although Gary saw all of that in the first glance, what really attracted his attention was Ann's smile. It seemed to glow with the sparkle in Ann's eyes and tied together with lips which were much redder than Gary had noticed before.

"Welcome to my little home. I live here alone. It is not fixed up exactly as I would like. I am working on it a little at a time."

"It looks great to me."

Gary was right. The apartment did look great. There was a light blue, solid-patterned carpet on the floor. The walls were a light shade of pink. There were some pictures on the wall, which Gary did not look at closely at first. It was Ann that was the sight which attracted his attention.

Gary was standing in a reasonably good-sized room. There was a table just off the center of the room to his left. On it was a pink tablecloth, two plates, silverware, and to one side, two single candles in single crystal candle holders. The candles were not lighted. There were two dark wood chairs, without upholstered seats, pulled up to the now set table, not across from each other, but at right angles to each other on two sides of the table. The chairs faced away from the door Gary had just entered.

To Gary's right there was a large white overstuffed chair facing a TV. There was a small table next to the chair, with a table lamp with a pink shade towards the back of this table.

"If you will help me bring the food in from the kitchen, everything is ready."

"I would rather look at you."

"I planned on everything being warm and ready. Do not distract me. I want to serve things the way I planned."

Gary followed Ann through a swinging door into the kitchen.

Ann handed Gary a hot plate, picked up two more plates, one in each hand, and led Gary back to the living room, turning as she entered and backing into the swinging kitchen door to push it open. Gary passed in front of her closely enough to have touched, but he did not bump into Ann. The plates were placed on the table. Gary held a chair for Ann. She sat down and smiled. Gary sat next to her on Ann's right.

Gary was a little speechless. There on those plates were the things he liked best. He wondered how Ann would know what his favorites might be. He wondered if she had called his mother to find out.

"I did not know what your favorite foods were. I just guessed. Did I make a good guess?"

"Very good. This is just the kind of steak I like best. The potatoes—do they call them twice mashed?—with cheese on the top are what I would fix for myself if I knew how."

"If you want, I can teach you."

"Not tonight. I could never make them this light and fluffy. The small green peas are my favorites also."

"The salad is what my mother used to make. I do not think I can do better than she."

"It would be hard to improve on this."

The food was so good one would be tempted to eat and not talk, but the company was also very good. There was a mixture of eating and visiting. Nothing was said about the article nor the subjects they had discussed at the office. Although their acquaintance was not extensive and the subjects they had discussed were limited, they did not seem to be speechless or pause to think of anything to say. The dinner was very congenial.

"Ann, do not feel insulted. I should only be looking at you, as pretty as you look all the time, especially right now, but those pictures on the wall intrigue me. Did you paint them?"

"How could you guess that?"

"I see down in the lower right-hand corner last year's date, and the initials A.L."

"You must have good eyes. Yes, I painted those for my own amusement. I picked the colors in the pictures to match the colors I intended to use in this apartment. I like them."

"I like them, too. My eyes are good, especially when I am looking at something pretty that I like such as those pictures and my present dinner companion."

Ann thought she should say something for an answer. Before she could think of a good reply, it occurred to her that Gary was getting a little more proficient at flattery. She liked what Gary had said.

"You did not tell me, Ann, that you were an accomplished artist in addition to being an accomplished writer and a charming person."

Ann knew she had to ignore the flattery. "There are a lot of things I have not told you about myself."

"Should I hang around until I learn all of them?"

Ann did not answer.

"If I look at those paintings long enough, I think I will figure out the scene you are depicting. Are they at the state park?"

"Yes."

"I said you were good."

"You keep changing the subject on me. I have some dessert ready, too. Help me get it out of the refrigerator."

Gary followed Ann to the kitchen. The desert was green lime sherbet covered with thick chocolate fudge dressing and served already in two crystal goblets. They were on plates. Gary was very careful that the goblet did not slide off the plate. He followed Ann back to the table.

Congenial conversation followed. Gary did not mention the pictures or her artistic ability any more. There were a lot of other things to talk about.

Even the best meal with the very best companionship still has to come to an end. This one did. Gary had followed his mother's instructions. He had cleaned his plate, each plate.

As Ann stood up she started cleaning the table of the plates. Gary helped. He followed Ann to the kitchen.

"We will not clean up now or do the dishes. They can wait."

"I can do the dishes. My mother insisted I do that when I was at home."

"You mother raised a very polite and considerate son."

"She would be surprised to hear anyone say that. She thought there were a lot of things I could and should do better."

As Ann turned back towards the living room, Gary said, "When you invited me to come here, you made it very clear I was invited for dinner and nothing more. I have had a wonderful dinner. I have had more than that. I have had a very companionable evening. Does that mean I should leave now that dinner is over?"

"Don't be silly. You know what I meant. It is early. Besides that, I have something to show you."

"Is it going to be any more beautiful than what I have already seen tonight?"

"What have you seen tonight that is so beautiful?"

"You."

"Gary, you should not talk like that."

"At the office you said I should not say personal things because it was a business office. This is not a business office. It is your home. You can make the rules, but I want to say what I feel like saying when I feel like saying it. You look beautiful to me. I want to say so. Are you going to prevent my saying so?"

"No, you can say anything you want to say to me."

"You are smart, charming, and beautiful."

"You are not so bad yourself."

There was a pause by both. Neither knew exactly what was the proper thing to say now.

"Gary, sit in the big white chair. I have something else to show you."

In a few moments Ann came into the living room with a large white poster card. It had a sketch in pencil of six people standing, apparently staring at something which was not yet sketched in. There was a boy and a girl. There was a man and a lady. There was an older couple. The people in the picture were not all of the same color of skin. Ann showed the card to Gary.

"We agreed we would not discuss business or our article tonight."

"Yes."

"This is close to the subject of the article, but it is not so close as to violate our agreement. You remember we discussed prejudice and the fact that no one had the choice of their parents or the color of their skin, no one had a choice as to the gender they would have, and no had a choice as to when they would be born and, therefore, no choice as to their age. I wrote a little poem to say that because of this, everyone was alike."

"You wrote the poem. Yes, I remember."

"I wondered if I could make a drawing or painting that said the same thing. I sketched something as a start. This is it. I have a lot more to do on it."

"That is interesting. I have noticed at art galleries there is usually a little card hanging on the wall beside a painting which identifies the name and birth date of the artist and the material used in the painting such as 'acrylic on canvas.' Most of the time I wished the museum would also set out what the artist was trying to tell. I have decided most artists are not trying to tell something. They are trying to show something which is pretty.

"You are different. You are striving to show this idea. You write like this, too. You try to show, not tell. This is a great idea. It should be an interesting piece when it is finished."

"It will take me a long time to finish. Our article will be completed a long time before this is completed."

"Are you sketching someone you know?"

"How can you tell?"

"The young lady looks a lot like you."

"Is it good enough for you to recognize?"

"Am I wrong? Is not that a sketch of you?

"Yes, I intended it to be. I was going to sketch you as the young man, but I decided not to do that. To tell the story I wanted to tell, I wanted to make the young man have a different color of skin than the young lady. I must still have some prejudice because I did not want you and me not to be the same color."

"I guess I understand. I would be flattered to be with you in the painting even if I had a different color."

"Well, I will have a lot of time to work on this. It may not finish like it is now."

"Do you have any other unfinished pictures?"

"Yes, I experiment with different things. Just to see how I could do something, I have been working on a painting of myself. I believe it is called a self-portrait. Would you like to see it?"

"Of course."

"Wait while I get it."

Ann left the sketch leaning against the wall. She went to what Gary was assuming was the bedroom. She returned with a canvas mounted on a wooden frame, not yet with a picture frame. She showed that to Gary. It was a front view of Ann all right. There could be no mistake about that.

"One of the problems, Gary, in painting one's self, is that you are used to looking at yourself in a mirror, which is just reversed from what you look like in a photograph or to anyone else. Most people do not like their own photographs because of that difference. I have been using a photo of myself as a model. I did not like the photo, so I do not like this painting. My mother says the photo looks like me. She thinks this painting looks like me, too."

"She is right. It is a good likeness. You are pretty good, you know. That is a very good picture of a very lovely lady."

"I have no idea of what I am going to do with it."

"My birthday is exactly two weeks before your birthday."

"How do you know that?"

"I looked in your personnel file."

"Do you mean you can look in my personnel file, and I cannot look into yours?"

"I do not know if you can look into mine or not. If it makes any difference to you, it is not necessary to look into my file to tell how old I am. I was born four years before you were born."

"I did not ask that. What I want to know is if you are hinting you would like to have this picture of me for your birthday?"

"I like beautiful things."

Gary did not tell Ann that he also painted pictures as a hobby. His were not even close to being as good as Ann's paintings.

Ann thought what had been said was an answer. She did not know if she wanted Gary to have that picture to hang in his apartment. She would like to see the apartment first, so she would know how it would look there. Ann said no more.

Ann leaned this picture against the wall, facing Gary. She excused herself. She went to another room, which Gary assumed was the bathroom. She did whatever ladies do in the bathroom. She also freshened her lips with another coat of lipstick. She knew she was not used to wearing lipstick, but she thought the light was so low that maybe she should brighten her face a little.

When Ann returned she walked up to the big white chair facing the TV and stood there looking at Gary, who occupied the entire chair. Gary said, "I do not know if this chair is big enough for both of us. It is if we are well-enough acquainted." As Gary finished saying that, he reached and grabbed Ann behind her knees, pulling her onto his lap. "We can get better acquainted."

This was not one of Ann's planned events for the evening. It violated her directions to come for dinner and nothing more. Yet Ann did not resent what had happened. She wondered if she should be careful at reminding Gary of the "nothing more." She would exact in her own way her own penalty for his grabbing her and pulling her onto his lap.

Ann landed on Gary's lap with her face higher than Gary's face. Her lips were right opposite Gary's forehead. She saw her opportunity to teach Gary a lesson. Ann leaned forward. Deliberately, not from emotion or ideas of romance, she placed her lips on

Gary's forehead. Ann left her lips there long enough to make an impression. She left a big red mark the size and shape of her lips right there in the middle of Gary's forehead. She would not tell Gary the mark was there. He could not see it there unless he looked in a mirror. She would let him embarrass himself when someone else informed him it was there.

As Ann leaned back to examine her handiwork, Gary pulled Ann down to where his lips met her lips. He did this with some energy and emotion. He gathered some more lipstick around his mouth. Ann did not seem to mind this happening either. She could see the red being smeared. She would not tell Gary what was on his face. She wondered how much more she could place there. Ann proceeded to find out, using the only method she knew. They both found this was an interesting investigation which did improve acquaintance and did not require any words.

Their arms were in the way. This problem was solved by each placing their arms around the other.

Ann did not know what to say, so she said nothing. She was too busy to talk anyhow. Gary seemed to be very satisfied with whatever communication was being conveyed without words.

To complete her plan to tease Gary, Ann left more lipstick marks. She did not tell him they were there.

Just as the meal had been finished, time marched on.

"When I said you did not have to leave because the meal was finished, I did not mean you should stay all night. We both have work to do tomorrow."

"I think I will retire and quit my job. The job is not as interesting as this."

"Don't be silly. There will be other days and other evenings."

"I hope so."

Ann unfolded her arms. She pulled Gary's arms from her. She stood up. Gary pulled himself from the depths of the chair. He also stood. Ann reached for Gary's hand. She guided him to the door. Ann put both arms around Gary's neck. She pulled herself up and closer to him. She did not intend to smear her lipstick on his lips any more than she already had, but she did. Ann did not tell Gary about her mark on his forehead or the red about his mouth and face. She could see that anyone Gary might meet would notice.

"It is sure a lot more fun to say goodnight inside the front door than outside the door. The meal was wonderful. Your company was great. Thanks. Getting better acquainted was pretty good, too."

"I do not know how to say this, Gary. I am very glad you came here. It is fun to work with you. I think this was more fun. Goodnight."

Gary opened the door. He did not look back. He left with a big smile on his face and a lot of red, too.

# CHAPTER FIFTEEN

As was usual, Gary was the first one to arrive at the office. As was also usual, Ann was almost as early. No one else was in the work room when Gary went to Ann's desk, grabbed the same chair he had used before and sat astraddle of it again, getting that done before Ann sat down.

"Well, Ann, that was sure a delightful evening. I did not intend to spend the evening discussing our article. I am glad we did not. You are a pleasure to be with. Nevertheless, now it is time to get back to work."

The red was all gone. Gary said nothing about it. Gary had thought about the red. In fact, he thought of a little poem to go with her trick of covering his face with all those red lip marks. He recited the poem to himself. The poem went,

> Before I Could Go To Bed
> I Washed Off All That Red.
> I Did Not Know That Lipstick.
> Could Be Put On Quite That Thick.

Ann was wondering if Gary was returning her joke and teasing her by leaving her in suspense as to how her gag of covering him with her lip marks had worked out. She would never know if someone had teased Gary about the red, or if he had found it himself when he got home.

"Yes, Gary."

"I appreciate your listening to my confusion on what to say about a cure for the overcrowding of the planet. Your listening while I thought out loud got me all cleared up in my reasoning. I know now there is no problem for me with ethics, morality, religion, or the question 'Is this God's will?' when we are discussing birth prevention which is undertaken before viability."

"Before viability, there is no life to terminate. I believe I will have no trouble writing these ideas. I am sure it will be easier to say those things than to convince those who somehow have thought such activity was the same as killing."

"Yes, Gary, there will be some problems convincing those who do not want to be convinced."

"I have decided to write this from the position of logic alone. I will discuss religion and morality and the health of the mother in more detail than should be necessary, just to be sure the subject is covered. I want anyone reading this to, at least, be presented with a rational logical presentation. Whether anyone will want to understand or be convinced is another matter."

Gary had not asked Ann a question. His statement did not call for a response. Ann did not feel she could remain silent. She said, "Gary, I, too, thought last night was a delightful evening at my apartment. I am glad also we did not spend all evening discussing our article and business.

"Now, about our discussion of the article, I do not recall anything I did or said, even just listening, that would unconfuse you—if there is such a word as 'unconfuse.' Perhaps getting away from the subject and relaxing let your subconscious mind straighten you out if you were confused. Whatever it was, I am glad you feel better about the subject this morning. You sound more at ease. I would say you look better this morning, too."

Gary said to himself, *I ought to look better this morning. I am wearing my best suit, shirt, and tie, and I got a hair cut. I wonder why I did that this morning?* Out loud, Gary said, "Well, I am more at ease about the project, but I am not completely at ease. Other matters, which I will not mention right now, confuse me. I will get back to writing about what does not confuse me. Instead of meeting at one o'clock, can we meet at noon and I take you to lunch?"

"You are incorrigible. Get back to work. Let me get back to work. Of course, I will enjoy your company at lunch, but it should be a lunch where each of us pays for our own meal."

# CHAPTER SIXTEEN

At lunch Ann said, "The other day you said something about the Old Testament which made me think you did not believe it was as good an authority as the New Testament. I do not understand what you meant."

"Well, I did not mean too much. I have not spent a lot of time thinking about that. What I was driving at is the Old Testament contains the sayings of prophets and wise men which were spoken before Jusus was born. I consider that Jesus was the son of God. I consider what Jesus said to be of much greater authority than what was said in the Old Testament."

"We should not ignore the Old Testament. It is part of the Bible."

"Yes, but, for example, if abortion or causing a miscarriage was such a horrible matter of which God did not approve, you would think, since it is in the Old Testament, that Jesus would have said something about it or explained what is in the Old Testament. Then we would know what the word of God on abortion might be."

"You do not find that Jesus ever discussed miscarriage or abortion or even avoiding child birth?"

"No. I have asked some people who I would think would know if there was discussion of those issues in the Bible anywhere."

This was lunch hour. More business was not discussed. It was getting so they did not have a subject to discuss. They could start and keep a conversation going just on the excitement of being together.

# CHAPTER SEVENTEEN

As usual, it was Ann who was the first to open the business discussion after they had returned from lunch. She did not start with small talk. She said, "Of all the things that have been said and could be said on the matter of birth prevention, we have omitted one matter that has probably been said the most of all. 'It is against God's will.'"

Gary scratched his head, put down the draft, and replied, "You are correct. We mentioned that as a problem to consider, but we did not say anything about it in our discussion. How will we discuss God's will? Who knows what God's will may be? How do we find out what is God's will on this when nothing is said in the Bible about it? One thing is sure. If no one can show from the Bible what God's will on abortion may be one way or the other, no one can say that abortion is against God's will."

Ann replied, "I do not know what God's will may be. I just know that some people sometimes, perhaps even frequently, use such an argument to justify what it is they do, want to do, or do not want to do."

Gary started to think out loud again. He said, "A problem in knowing what God's will may be is that different people in different parts of the world worship different gods. The different gods have different philosophies. Probably, therefore, God's will varies with the god that is being worshipped at the time and with the worshippers."

"That makes it very difficult to discuss."

"God's will has undoubtedly been the subject of a lot of discussion by a lot of different people. The answers would vary directly according to the number of people who have exercised their conjecture on this subject. I would guess there would be a problem in discussing what the will of God may be in the church where my parents took me and where I went in the days when I did go to Sunday School and church more than I do now."

"Gary, I do not know what church, if any, you went to or whether you still go. You may or may not have ideas based upon what you learned in your church."

"I still go to church. I probably do not go as often as I should go. Do you?"

"Since I have lived here and worked on this paper, I have gone to church less than I did when I was living at home and when I was going to college. I do not know the people in the church here. It is not as much fun-or interesting, if that is a better term-to go alone. At home I went to a friendly church where everyone talked to each other and where they no longer frown on playing cards, dancing, or even having a little drink occasionally. I play cards; I dance. I have not gotten around to drinking yet although I do not think it is the church which has anything to do with my not drinking."

"That is about the same situation with me. I have been out of college and living alone long than you have. I just have not felt the need to go to church although I know I should."

"Ann, to tell you right now and be accurate about what I learned concerning what may be the will of God is difficult."

Ann then said, "The minister of my church once told me the Christian religion is a negative religion. The Christian religion preaches what not to do and not much about what to do. I recall my minister saying there were portions of the Bible where Jesus is reported as telling people what to do, such as loving God and treating your neighbor as yourself. Right now I do not recall being told or reading what Jesus said about what might be the will of God."

"I do not believe that there is anything in the Bible about God's will concerning birth prevention. As I said before, I do not think Jesus said anything about it at all."

"That is interesting. That is about the same information and feeling that comes to my mind at this moment. Maybe we can figure out something. Gary, what do people mean when they say, in reference to prevention of birth, that it is against God's will?"

Gary said, "I can answer, I think. They use the expression 'God's will' to explain that they think God does not want people to interfere with or change life from what would happen naturally without action by man. Do you have any different idea, Ann?"

"No. That is about all I think they could mean, but what is it that happens naturally without the action of man? In animals we could attribute the birth process to instinct. However, animals are not thinking beings who have control over their actions. Animals go where food and water is no matter what the obstacle may be. They can be captured by bait of food. They can be enticed into the range of the hunter by what they believe is a call for a mate. Animals can be driven and manipulated by man."

"Yes, I agree with that."

"But human beings have great control over their actions. Man's actions are governed by thoughts, motives, and desires. Man can and does make choices as to what he consumes and where he goes. Man has a choice to pick his own mate and to procreate or not to procreate as he determines. Customs and habits may influence people, but humans can control their own activities."

"Ann, you are about to say that with humans, things do not actually come naturally. You are saying everything man does, is the act of man and not the act of God. You are saying man can act contrary to the will of God."

"Yes, I was trying to figure out how to say that. Man does a lot of things which change the earth and the way we live, which could not be said to have come naturally. Man cuts down the trees to make fields. He plows up the natural foliage, plants other things, cultivates the fields to kill the weeds, which are just other plants which man does not want right there. Man uses fertilizers to make more plants grow bigger. Man uses insecticides to kill the insects man does not want to consume his crops.

"Man does a lot of things to avoid wind erosion and water erosion. He uses soil conservation procedures to protect the soil from the elements. Man irrigates to provide more moisture for the crops than comes naturally. Men shave and ladies use makeup. There are a lot of things we do which are not just 100 percent natural."

"Yes, Ann. The world does not seem to have been damaged by those, at least. It cannot be said man lets the earth go naturally. If man had done that, long ago we would have reached the food production shortage we envision for the future."

"Yes."

"God does not seem displeased with how man has protected the earth from erosion-both wind and water. I would think God did not expect that man would let the earth go 'naturally.'"

"I am surprised a little, Gary, that you, the big tough editor, can be so profound. You are right. Man does have the capability of doing what is against the will of God. There are a lot of things being done by man to each other, to the world, and to the environment, that I would hope are contrary to the will of God."

"The biggest trouble in discussing this, Ann, is we do not know and do not know how to discover what may actually be the will of God." Without any interruption, Gary followed with, "It would seem reasonable to assume that God does want man to use the mental capacity and abilities which God gave to him to determine when and how he shall act. It would seem to be a reasonable conclusion that if God did not want man to use such ability, God would not have given that ability to man. God did not make man to be just another animal. God must have, as part of his will, expected and wanted man to protect and preserve the things which God has provided. That would include, of course, all of the resources of the planet, the animals, the plants, the air, the water, the sunshine, and everything else which God has provided."

Ann was quiet for a while before she said, "Geology has taught us the earth has changed over the ages without the intervention of man. Rivers have changed their courses. Mountains have appeared where none first existed. The countryside has been eroded by wind and water. All sorts of changes have occurred which the geologists describe, all without man and all, therefore, in the sole control of God. It would seem, therefore, it would not be against God's will for there to be changes in the planet. It is also probable it does not displease God that there have been changes made in the earth with the intervention of man."

"You are correct, Ann. It logically follows that it would please God, and it would be God's will for man to do something to preserve the planet, to act to ensure its survival, and to promote its prosperity."

Gary continued the reasoning they had started, "Of course, it would please God and be God's will for man to take some action aside from letting things go without any thought or action by man. It would please God to protect and preserve what God has provided, including all of the things necessary to assure the planet's survival and its prosperity."

"I like your reasoning, Gary. That is what we are engaged in at the moment."

"God lets floods and droughts exist and vary. God provides for the preservation and improvement of breeds of animals. God lets the weaker animals starve when the food resources are insufficient and when animals become so overcrowded that the resources existing naturally do not provide enough sustenance for so many animals. These methods of evolution must be a part of God's will."

Ann, being swept up in the sequence of conclusions running logically from the ideas each of them had discussed, hurried on by saying, "So, it would seem God would be pleased, and it would be God's will to see man take the same type of steps with the size of his family which God takes with the animals to provide that the population of man does not exceed the ability of the earth to provide for the human race. In other words, it is probable that it would please God and be God's will for each person to arrange for himself or herself control over the size of the part of the human population with which each person has some control by his voluntary and considered action in preventing more births than the world can support."

"As a matter of fact," said Gary, "it might be against God's will if the human race does not provide for the survival and continuation of the human race in comfort and prosperity by limiting the size of the human race to what the earth can support."

"You have just said it is God's will that man prevent birth."

"I have heard it said, in church and elsewhere, that God helps those who help themselves. God expects man to arrange his affairs to fit the earth's resources."

"You did not ask if I agreed," Ann interrupted, "but the logic which we have just expressed is very compelling."

"There is still the possibility that both of us are wrong. We must realize that. It must also be God's will that, when each person tries to protect the earth and the resources which God has provided, God contemplates that we will make mistakes. Nonetheless, I feel sure it is God's will that we try to protect the planet."

"Someone, I do not remember who, said something like this: 'I would rather try and fail than not try and succeed.' I believe that is God's will, too."

"I have always enjoyed such thinking."

# CHAPTER EIGHTEEN

As Gary and Ann approached the door to Ann's apartment after a nice dinner together and a lot of visiting, Gary wondered if he would be invited to come in. Ann handed Gary the keys. Gary unlocked the door, handed the keys back to Ann, opened the door, and stood back.

Gary handed something to Ann as Ann started to enter the apartment. Gary said, "Use this."

Ann looked at what Gary had handed to her. She immediately saw it was a lipstick tube. She checked the end of the tube. She found it to be the same brand and the same shade of red with which she had marked Gary when he came to the apartment for dinner. Ann smiled. She reached for Gary's hand and guided him through the door. When they were both inside, Ann closed the door and turned on the lights.

Then she turned to Gary, raised up on her toes, put her arms around his neck, and pulled Gary's head down to her face. She carefully placed her lips on his lips. She forced herself against him. Gary responded to each motion of Ann's with a similar motion of his own. They lingered. They did not speak. They were already conveying the message each of them wanted to send to the other.

Then Ann stretched upwards. She moved her lips from Gary's lips to his forehead. She carefully placed her lips there as if to give him another brand.

"I do not have time to wait to put on lipstick. You know I do not usually wear lipstick, unless I want to look gaudy, as I did the other night, or unless I want to play a trick on you, as I did the other night. Tonight I do not want to look gaudy. Tonight I do not want to play a trick on you. Tonight I wanted to do what we just did. Was what I just did without lipstick as good as what I did the other night with lipstick?"

"Better. There was no delay tonight. I think you put more feeling into it this time. You were not playing a trick on me."

"Don't be too sure about that. It may not be just the same trick."

"This trick I will not have to wash off."

"Do you want to wash it off?"

"No, I need another application."

Gary did not wait for Ann to paint another coat with her moist but not red kiss. He placed one of his own right on her lips where he wanted it. Ann carefully applied whatever there was to apply.

After a little more of that exchange Ann dropped off of her toes. She led Gary to the big white chair. She pushed Gary down into the chair. She climbed onto his lap. Ann applied some more of her affection. Gary replied in kind.

"I know, Ann, when I was invited here for dinner and nothing more, I didn't follow my instructions. I disobeyed you. I reached for you. I took more. You had a right to play a trick on me for that. I thought we were both enjoying the 'more.' I did not know you were applying your mark. But I liked it. I wondered if I furnished the branding iron, so to speak, in the form of more lipstick, if you would brand me again. From what I saw when I got home, I could not see how you could have had any lipstick left. I wanted to be sure there was some."

"How did you know this was the same brand and shade of red?"

"I am an investigative journalist. I do not reveal my sources or my investigative techniques."

"I will not reveal mine either."

"Thanks. I am not sure it is an improvement to do things my way."

"You do not need to bring anything for me to apply to you. I will manufacture my own."

So saying, Ann moistened her lips. She then applied a moist deposit on the end of Gary's nose.

"You missed."

"No, I did not miss. I never make a mistake like that. You were supposed to fence that one off to where you wanted it. I can be managed if you try, but do not try any more management tonight."

Gary did not know what that was supposed to mean, but he did not care. He saw to it that her lips went to the right place.

"You know, Gary, I have you where I can control you whenever I want. You are my immediate superior at my place of employment. You are a big strong handsome man. I am a weak manageable woman. When you go one instant beyond my permission, I can see you in court for sexual harassment."

"Have I reached that point yet?"

"No, but you are getting close."

"Is it that bad? Is it getting that late?"

"It is getting close."

"I would rather see you in the office and here than see you in court."

So saying, they expressed themselves again, forcefully. Ann twisted herself away. She started to get out of the chair without letting their lips separate. That was difficult to do, which caused her to fall back to where she had been. They repeated their efforts. Ann unfolded her arms, removed her lips, and did get up. She walked to the door. She stood there until Gary came close. They repeated, without saying a word, what they had done when they first came into the apartment that night.

# CHAPTER NINETEEN

Morning came, as mornings are in the habit of doing. Ann and Gary were back at their desks again. The Bible was still there.

Everything was all business.

Discussing prevention of birth was the hardest part of what they planned to do. It was difficult because of the original confusion and prejudice they each had. It was also their desire to be objective and perhaps to convince those who did not want to be convinced. They both realized a revision and a rewrite would be necessary. They had discussed some subjects more than once. Birth prevention was not the only factor that needed to be mentioned concerning the survival of the planet.

"There is one other thing, Gary, that must be considered before we write this up as our conclusion."

"What is it?"

"How does abortion fit into the Biblical injunction to 'be fruitful and multiply'?"

"I am not a Bible expert, Ann. That statement appears in the Old Testament, in Genesis when the earth was being created. At that time the earth needed population. It does not need more population now. That statement may not have been intended as religious instruction. It was good advice at the time of the formation of the earth. Did God intend that particular injunction to be religious advice or advice fitting the population needs of the earth at the time in which it was said? Would God give the same instructions to us now that the earth is overflowing as he gave when the earth was empty?"

"It would not seem logical that God would do that."

"Ann, you seem to be more familiar with the scriptures than I. However, if I remember, that direction to be fruitful and to multiply does not appear to be a direct instruction from God or Jesus concerning human population."

"Yes, Gary, that is my recollection. It is in the Old Testament, so Jesus could not have said that."

"Those passages have been translated from the language in which the Old Testament was written, into Greek, and then into English. I am not sure the translation is sufficiently clear and unambiguous that it should be followed in times which are different from when it was said. I do not believe the direction is sufficiently certain to let us disregard what appears to be clear about the will of God."

"I am not certain, but I believe it is possible that some of the statements in the Bible were intended as economic advice instead of religious advice. I am not, however, confident enough to write that as part of our article."

"I was not saying what we should put in our article. I was just thinking out loud about the situation. It helped me to analyze my conflicting ideas and emotions. I was in hope you would disagree and dispute me. You are too nice."

"No, Gary, I am not too nice. I am stubborn when I know I am right, but on these things we have been discussing, I am not sure about what is right and what is wrong."

"It is too bad we have to reach some finality in writing our article. I will say one thing though. It has been fun discussing this with you. I have never had to answer these questions before. You probably have not had to answer them, either. At least I am more informed now than I was before. I understand other people's ideas and emotions better."

"Gary, you have expressed my feelings and my doubts, too. Why don't you write up something on the 'will of God,' 'thou shalt not kill,' and 'be fruitful and multiply.' We can see how it looks and feels when written down. I will work on something else. We will revise together. It would not be God's will for us to waste time, which is one of the resources God has given to us."

# CHAPTER TWENTY

Now those of us who are reading this and who eavesdropped and watched when they wrote the conclusions of the conversations in which these ideas developed would understand the uncertainty. We might notice that some of the conversations on company time were not precisely relevant to the article. We would not have concluded Gary and Ann were adversaries, friendly or otherwise. We would have concluded they were very businesslike in trying to reach conclusions on troublesome matters which they encountered.

We would have observed they continually concluded that survival depended upon prosperity. They each had different ideas about what would be the best way to arrive at continual prosperity. Their differences here, however, were not based upon doubts and uncertainties like those which existed in trying to understand God's will, etc.

They decided that even though they differed on the means, they agreed on the end. They considered that, with research and accomplishments based on research and knowledge, there would not need to be a decision on what was the 'will of God' nor on the directions 'thou shalt not kill'and 'be fruitful and multiply.' If there was enough prosperity spred among all of the people, it would be possible for each person to make his own decisions on 'the will of God,' 'thou shalt not kill,' be fruitful and multiply,' and many other things upon which persons of good will could reasonably disagree.

Ann and Gary did conclude that the decisions on these matters were personal. Everyone would have to understand the right of each person to make his own decisions. Forcing someone to accept the views of someone else was not right, was not part of the will of God, and would not work.

However, Ann and Gary could see that birth prevention was not the entire answer to survival and prosperity.

# CHAPTER TWENTY-ONE

Ann and Gary discussed all these things and argued, not too vigorously, about how to place these important matters in their article.

We also noticed that Gary and Ann were spending alot of time together apparently working and conducting business.

We could observe that some of the other employees were begining to comment that Ann and Gary were becoming a twosome.

We would not observe Gary and Ann coming to work together in the morning. No one else was around that early in the morning. We might notice them at lunch together. The other employees would leave at quitting time. They would see Ann and Gary still there, apparently working.

The other employees would not notice that Gary and Ann also ate together each evening. Sometimes evenings were spent at places which were fancier than the first restaurant at which they ate together. Sometimes they were dressed up more than they were at work.

The other employees would not have observed that Ann and Gary occasionally went to a show or went dancing. Nor would they have observed that frequently Ann invited Gary to her apartment. They would not have an opportunity to learn that Ann was a very good cook. They would only have been able to guess that Ann was working on the premise that the way to a man's heart was through his stomach.

Those of us who are reading this would have had to speculate as to what, if anything other than the article, was being developed.

We could safely guess that with each passing day there was realization that the entire completion of the article was nearer. We could also guess there was some hesitation due to thinking that finishing the article might end the need for this continual association. It was, after all, a delightful combination of both opportunity and temptation.

In approaching the finish, decisions had to be made to leave something as it was instead of doing another rewrite. They could rewrite forever.

# CHAPTER TWENTY-TWO

"Ann, before we finish, there are two other things which I have heard about which we have not discussed but which should be in the article."

"What are they?"

"We mentioned the overcrowding in poor countries, the death of children from starvation, and the malnutrition of adults and, therefore, their early deaths. The resistance to birth control and abortion in those countries just makes the situation worse. When there is not enough food, the children will be the last to be fed. The children will die.

"Everyone agrees that killing someone already born or in the period of viability is wrong."

"Yes, Gary. It seems that the prejudice against abortion and resistance to it is actually causing the deaths of some of those already born through over consumption of the scarce food supply. That is also killing people. Why did I not see that when I was opposed to abortion? You will recall I was opposed to abortion when we started working together on this article. This article helps me. I hope it helps others. I would rather help save children and people who are already born than save fetuses which have not reached viability. Apparently, we cannot do both."

"There is one other thing we should consider and perhaps put in our article, Ann."

"You mean there is something else we have left out?"

"Yes, some people think there is an epidemic which is bringing the disease of AIDS to more and more people. Many people have died of AIDS, and more will die of AIDS. There has not yet been discovered a cure. Up until now the best advice that doctors can give is to try to prevent exposure to AIDS. They say that abstinence is the best prevention but at the same time seem to be saying they know people are not going to follow abstinence. They recommend, as a better alternative to having unprotected sexual conduct, the use of condoms."

Oh, my goodness. Aids seems to get into too many conversations. Yes, I remember, that is one of the things which is most recommended for AIDS avoidance."

"The trouble is that condoms are also a universally used method—of avoiding conception." Those people who oppose use of birth prevention methods believe that use of birth control methods is sinful. They therefore do not believe people should use condoms for any reason.

"The result is that the so-called religious ideas against conception are actually preventing the use of the best known means of avoiding becoming infected with AIDS."

"AIDS is so horrible, Gary."

"Treatment for AIDS is so expensive, even though it is ineffective, that AIDS must be one of the factors which threatens both the survival and prosperity of the earth."

"Yes, I see what you are saying."

"Most victims of AIDS do not have enough funds to pay for the treatment which is available now. So the cost of treatment, which is very high, is paid from welfare funds or the funds paid by uninfected people for their health insurance premiums. That means it is paid by taxpayers or increases in the nation's fiscal deficit. When those expenses are paid by insurance, all policy holders are paying for the AIDS treatment."

"Does that mean, Gary, that the prejudice, religious or otherwise, against the use of birth prevention methods with the prejudice against killing of unborn children, results in avoiding the birth control methods which would prevent infection from AIDS? Does it follow, therefore, that oposition to abortion, which is based upon the idea that abortion is the killing of unborn persons, actually results in the killing of people who have already been born?"

"Yes, it seems that way. Some people are going to die or not be conceived before birth by using birth prevention tools. Some people are going to die of AIDS after birth by not using the condom birth prevention tool."

"That is a dilemma that ought to help convince anyone to abandon his prejudice against birth control. I see what you are saying, Gary. That medical expense affects the prosperity of everyone. The money spent on such medical matters or welfare or insurance premiums affects the prosperity of the world."

"Ann, do you realize what we have just concluded?"

"What are you going to say now?"

"The religious objection to avoiding conception, 'birth prevention' we decided to call it, including abortion, is a big factor and danger to the survival and prosperity of the world. It helps create too many children for the economy to support, and it helps prevent use of one of the most effective methods of avoiding the epidemic that is killing people."

"No, Gary, it is not a religious objection which is the danger. It is prejudice against abortion which is the danger. We have pretty well established that the objection to abortion is not based on anything in the Bible, and therefore, it is not a religious objection. The danger is the prejudice which has no foundation in the Bible."

"Ann, you have just said that the church which opposes abortion is a big danger to both the survival and prosperity of the world."

"I did not intend to say that."

"What else is the conclusion from what you said?

Ann was quiet for a long time. Gary did not interrupt her contemplation. Ann quietly said, "I do not like the conclusion I reached. It seems, however, to be accurate. Do you reach the same conclusion?"

"Yes."

"What do we do now?"

"If we are honest journalists, as we have to be, that conclusion will have to be a part of our article. God will forgive us for telling the truth."

"Oh my! That will be making a startling and controversial statement. I did not expect our article would be a troublemaker. What will Burner say?"

Gary replied, "When, I say 'when' instead of 'if,' we put this in our article, Burner can be mad. He can take it out, but we will have done our duty to tell the truth as we see it."

"I can see the controversial things that will be printed and spread by TV, newspapers, and radio."

"Our job is not to avoid controversy. Stimulating thought on this matter of prejudice, not only regarding birth prevention, but prejudice because of race, gender, age and all other prejudices based on misconception of facts, is our job. We will be doing a service to the nation and the world."

"Yes, Gary, that has to be said. I am not reluctant now to write what we have just concluded."

# CHAPTER TWENTY-THREE

Late on the afternoon of the last thursday before the expiration of the time limit fixed by Burner, Gary looked over the draft which then exhisted. He made some changes. He took the draft with the changes, to Ann. Ann had' another copy of the draft. She also had made some changes. When they compaired their copies, they discovered the changes each had made were amazingly similar.

Their manuscript set out in logical order all the observations that they had made in their discussions. It 'recited' all the conclusions they had reached as they had thought out loud together about all of these matters. Step by step the manuscript showed the relation and interdependence that survival and prosperity have to each other. It especially showed the danger of prejudice to the survival and prosperity of the world.

They thought that anyone reading the manuscript would have to come to the conclusion that there were things which should be done now to assist survival and attain or retain prosperity. The things they both emphasized were the dangers of prejudice and of overpopulation of the planet.

They expressed their reluctant conclusions that birth planning and prevention, including abortion, were tools now needed or soon to be desperately needed to continue both survival and prosperity.

Both Ann and Gary concluded that public dissention over the abortion issue was destructive to both survival and prosperity.

They concluded that abortion was not a religious issue at all. They decided that abortion was now an economic issue. It was the best way to accomplish survival and prosperity, along with education, increased productivity arriving through universal education, democratic free government, and care to not overuse the planet which God had provided.

Both Ann and Gary were now satisfied with their conclusions. They were proud of the way the conclusions had been reached. They were happy with the product of their efforts set out in the manuscript. They felt that any reasonable person would eliminate prejudice and would agree.

They believed, that if their conclusions were accepted, they had done something to improve the lives of everyone and to ensure the survival and prosperity of the planet.

After the review, Gary started the conversation "This article is good. These changes are good. We will probably find other changes we would like to make. I suspect we can redraft and revise forever. Burner did not ask for perfection, but he did ask that we have this done for publication in thirty days. Monday will be the thirtieth day."

"Yes, we can revise over and over. Maybe the revisions will be better. Maybe they will not be better."

"I am inclined to think we should stop right now. Tomorrow we can get to the point at which we have something finished to present to Burner as our final draft."

"It is always nice to finish on time. It is better to finish ahead of time if the quality of the work is good. This is good. We should stop now."

Ann continued, "I will say one thing about the draft which we now have. You and I have written so nearly alike and in the same style, I doubt if anyone will be able to tell which part of the article you wrote and which part I wrote. That, in itself, is an accomplishment."

# CHAPTER TWENTY-FOUR

Gary looked at Ann to see if she meant anything special in what she had just said. He decided she did not. Gary asked, "Do you want to go to dinner right now? I am hungry. Let's go some place nice."

Ann replied, "It is too late to start something new here at the office today. It is a good time to go to some place nice. I do not feel that I am dressed for something nice. Can we meet at my apartment? I will change quickly. If I get there first, I will leave the door ajar. You just come in and make yourself comfortable. If you get there first, wait for me. I do want to have you there. I have a special reason."

Ann looked pretty good to Gary just the way she was, but in the twenty-six days since he had started talking to Ann, he had learned it was not wise to suggest she looked fine when she wanted to look finer. He said, "You go on. I will be there soon."

When Gary arrived, the door to Ann's apartment was partly open. Gary went in. He called to Ann to tell her he had arrived. He asked her if he could use her bathroom. Ann was in the bedroom. She said, "You know where it is. You have been here enough to know you can be at home here."

Gary did not attach any special meaning to the statement.

When Gary was in the bathroom he dropped a towel. He decided to get a clean towel out of the drawer under the sink. Ann had said he should feel at home. When he opened the drawer, there on top of the towels was a man's electric shaver. Gary was surprised and shocked. During all of this time Gary had been working so closely with Ann, had Ann been seeing another man? Had that man been so welcome and at home as to bring his electric shaver? Did he leave it there because he was used to coming back and staying long enough to need a shave? Did he stay overnight?

Gary did not realize he could be jealous. He did not think clearly. He just got mad.

Gary took the shaver out of the drawer. He was carrying it to the living room when Ann came out of the bedroom wearing a robe, heading for the bathroom. Gary asked, "Which one of your boyfriends left this after he spent the night here with you?"

Ann's answer was a quick hard slap to the side of Gary's face. The slap covered his ear, stung his face, made his ear ring, and hurt his feelings. Gary grabbed Ann's wrist. Ann exclaimed, "Don't you ever make a statement like that to me again. This is my apartment. I am over twenty-one. I can entertain anyone I want here whether it is a man or not. You do not have any rights here or over me. You do not have any right to talk to me like that. I should not bother to explain. I should just ask you to leave. That shaver belongs to my father. He was in town. He came here to wait for his plane. He must have shaved and then forgotten it. I found it this morning. I intended to mail it to him, but I have not had a chance."

Ann was furious, but she also was a little pleased to find Gary was jealous. She knew he would not be jealous if he did not care for her. Ann decided to continue this demeanor of being furious. It was genuine.

Neither said anything until Gary spoke. "I apologize. I should not have been looking in your drawer for a towel. I should have thought better. Even if I did not think better, I should have kept my mouth closed. What can I do to apologize better and to straighten this out?"

"Nothing," Ann answered. "That was a terrible accusation to make of me."

Ann turned, went into the bathroom, and closed the door with a slam.

Gary did not know whether he should leave or wait. He decided to sit and wait. He heard the sound of the shower from the bathroom. After due time Ann came out in her robe, looked at Gary with bitter contempt, said nothing, went into the bedroom, and slammed the door. Gary continued to sit and wait.

After what seemed like an unreasonable length of time, Ann came out of the bedroom, dressed but not dressed up particularly. She wore no lipstick this time. She said, "I am still hungry, but you spoiled the chance for me to enjoy a dressed up dinner in a nice place. Where do you want to go?"

By this time Gary was standing. He approached Ann. Gary placed his right hand on her left shoulder. He said, "I am truly sorry I lost my temper. I will behave. Go back in there and put on a nice dress for a nice place."

Ann suddenly felt sorry she had slapped Gary. She wished she had not acted so violently. Ann took Gary's hand which was on her shoulder, moved it around to her back, reached up, and placed her lips on Gary's cheek. She said, "I am sorry I slapped you. You should not have thought or said what you said, but I should not have slapped you, either. I hope I did not hurt your ear. If you want more of an apology, you may return a better kiss than I just gave to you."

Already having one arm around Ann, it was not awkward to put the other arm around her, too, to pull Ann up closer, and to place his lips on her lips with some force and emotion. Ann did not turn or push Gary away. Ann put her arms around Gary's neck.

Ann responded with something only Ann and Gary could describe. As this event occurred, Ann rose on her toes, and then while her arms were holding around Gary's shoulder and while Gary's arms continued to encircle Ann, Ann dropped her weight back upon her heels, which overbalanced Gary. They both started to fall. They did not fall. They were both propelled closer to each other.

They lingered there while each assembled his or her thoughts or feelings, whichever it was at the moment. Ann then leaned back, looked in Gary's face, smiled, and returned to her former position. Gary, having enthusiasm, met the return. Shortly he, too, leaned back. He looked into Ann's eyes. They both smiled. Together they returned to each other.

How long this lasted could not have been measured. By a watch, it was probably less time than it appeared to Ann and to Gary. The event lingered. Neither relinquished his or her grasp.

Eventually Gary reached for and held Ann's hand as he led her over to the big white chair in front of the TV. He sat down. Gary gently pulled Ann onto his lap. Her arms returned to around his shoulders. Gary's arms returned to around her waist. Each snuggled as close to the other as they could. Communication without words commenced.

Some things take longer than others, but all events between active persons reach a point where there is a change. Without moving her head from Gary's shoulder, Ann said, "I have changed my mind. I do not want to go out to eat tonight. I wonder if there is anything appealing in the refrigerator. Come help me."

They arose from the chair. They went together to the kitchen, holding hands as they walked. They looked in the refrigerator and the cupboard. The cupboard was not bare, but it was not far from being bare. There was only a can of pork and beans and a jar of applesauce. Ann asked, "Have you ever had a dinner of beans and applesauce? It is not what I had in mind for this evening."

"I will take you some place."

"No, I do not feel like going out now. I feel like staying here with you. You do want to stay here with me, don't you?"

"Of course."

"Well, we will make do with what we have. You can help. You set the table. I will make coffee and put the beans in the microwave. Do you want your applesauce hot or cold?"

Gary did not answer. He just acted. It was her apartment. When he was there he would do what Ann wanted to be done there. He had already made a mistake tonight. The lipstick smeared on his forehead the first night he had been in the apartment had taught him a lesson, too.

Gary got two plates, two forks, two spoons, and two paper napkins. He also found two glasses, which he filled with ice cubes. He put two cups and saucers on the small kitchen table. He pulled up two chairs.

Ann found two candles and two candlesticks. She handed those to Gary, together with a book of paper matches. Gary put the candles in the candlesticks. Gary put the candlesticks on the table at the side, not where he would have to look around or through the flame of the candles to see Ann, or to have her look to see him. Gary lighted the candles. He turned off the overhead kitchen light.

Ann emptied the warm beans and the cold applesauce into separate bowls. She set them on the table. Then Ann went to the coffee maker.

When Ann returned to the table, Gary was holding Ann's chair for her to sit down. Ann did. As she did so, Ann looked up at Gary and smiled not only with her lips, but with her eyes and her whole countenance.

The candlelight reflected in Ann's eyes, enhancing the already dancing sparkle.

Gary had once taken a course in art appreciation. What he saw now was more beautiful than anything he had ever imagined. Gary looked down upon her face, moved closer, and leaned down as Ann leaned up. Their lips met and lingered while they remained in this awkward position.

The meal was surprisingly good. It is not the food which makes a meal great. It is the atmosphere and the companionship. The atmosphere was excellent. The companionship could never be matched.

Meals also end. Gary pulled back Ann's chair. She arose. Ann picked up the dishes and stacked them in the sink.

As Gary blew out the candles. Ann reached for Gary's hand. She led him back to the big chair in front of the TV. They resumed their previous positions and communications.

After a time, which may have seemed short or may have actually been short, Ann said, "I had planned on going out with you to dinner tonight, or soon, to a nice place. I bought a new dress solely to impress you with the fact that I can look different from just an office drudge. I also wanted to dress in such a way that you would realize I am a woman."

Gary replied, "I have noticed you are a lady. I have also noticed you are a very pretty lady. It would not take a new dress to cause me to notice or to be impressed."

"You certainly have not demonstrated you noticed. Do not try to flatter me. This is my idea to impress you. It was my idea to get and to wear a pretty dress when I was with you. Would you like to see it?"

So saying, but not waiting for an answer, Ann got up. She went to the bedroom. In a minute or so Ann was back carrying a blue dress, about knee length, hanging on a dress hanger.

"How do you like it?"

"On the hanger it looks very nice. How does it look on you?"

"Give me another minute. I will show you."

Gary stood up.

Off Ann went with the dress. Surprisingly it was not much more than another minute until Ann returned wearing the dress. It seemed to be the same color as the sky. However, it was not the color of the dress which grabbed Gary's immediate attention. The dress was kneecap length and had sleeves to just above the elbow, a high back, and a low front, a very low front. If the terminology of geography were used, one could say the dress showed the plains, all of the valley, and almost all the mountains on the valley's edge, with two peaks only barely concealed but very well suggested. What was suggested was very nice.

The view did not disclose what Gary called a "belly button, although the view seemed to go that far south. If it showed, Gary did not notice. His attention was elsewhere.

All of the visible topography was of the same natural skin color and smoothness that was a feature of Ann's face.

Ann was also wearing shoes that matched the color of the dress. They were open toed, high heeled, and graceful. Gary was too busy to notice the shoes.

Ann turned and swirled around, with the motion raising the skirt to a respectable sight. As Ann stopped the swinging, the skirt settled back down to where it had started. Ann asked, "Do you think it is too low in front?"

Before Gary could think of something tactful to say in response, Ann said, "I was in doubt about the depth of the cut in front, but I liked the dress. I wanted to impress you. I bought it to wear only when I am with you. I am not sure I want everyone to see this much of me. You are different. I feel comfortable with you."

Gary still did not know what to say. He used good judgment and said nothing. But Ann said, "You should quit staring. Look into my eyes. If I had known you were going to stare like that, I would have bought an old lady's dress. Do you want me to put a T-shirt over it?"

Gary laughed. He said, "I like it. It startled me. I was not expecting anything like this dress. I am not sure I want anyone else to see so much of you."

Ann said, "The front panels can be adjusted to the center, so the dress does not have to show this much. I just wanted to see how you would react when the panels were as far apart as they can go."

"Now you know how I responded. I hoped I acted properly."

Ann did not respond directly but said, "I have very little jewelry. Do you think I should put on a necklace?"

"Ann, you cannot improve on perfection. Do not wear anything else that will distract me from looking into your eyes."

Gary started to reach. Ann spun away. She said, "This is to look at, not to touch. If you will put your hands behind your back and keep them there, I will come a little closer."

Ann put her hands behind her back. Ann moved over to where Gary was standing. Both of them leaned forward. They touched each other only where silent personal communications of affection should be delivered.

When the gesture was finished, Ann said, "I bought something else to wear when I am with you. It is something you can both look at and touch if you want to touch. Would you like to see what else I bought?"

Knowing full well that Gary liked to see her and knowing also the no-touch rule while wearing the blue dress was going to be an impediment to the evening, Ann spun around twice, raising the skirt even higher. Ann wiggled her way to the bedroom, exaggerating her normal attractive stride and her movements for Gary.

Gary thought, "She looks as good going away as she does coming towards me."

"Will you come in here and unzip this dress? I got it on and zipped it up without any help, but I am having trouble finding the zipper tab at the top in back to zip it down. You can look but do not touch anything except the zipper."

Gary was having an evening of not knowing what to say or what to do after that one bad mistake. He was now using his best judgment in saying as little as possible. It was not necessary for Gary to say anything. Ann was guiding the situation very well, just as Gary would want. He did not see how he could improve on what had happened since his mistake.

Of course, he could touch enough to unzip the dress. He was hesitant.

"Never mind. If you are afraid to come here, I will get the dress unzipped all by myself."

She did. Had she needed Gary, or was she trying some ladies' wiles?

Gary was seated in the big chair facing the TV when Ann came out of the bedroom wearing a two piece slack suit. There was a white stretch blouse that fit as if it were her skin, with no apparent room between the blouse and Ann. Gary was afraid to help with the zipper on the blouse. Ann did not ask him to do so.

With the white blouse were black slacks which seemed to fit even tighter and closer to Ann than the blouse.

Although there was not as much bare skin as showed with the blue dress, this slack suit revealed even more than the dress suggested. With something that tight, there was no mystery left about Ann. What one could imagine from a glance was very nice.

The slacks reached down to a pair of black high-heeled patent leather shoes with heels much higher than Gary had observed Ann wearing. They were even higher than the red shoes she had worn the night that she branded Gary with her red. In fact, Ann did not balance very well on those ultra high-heels. Ann stumbled a little. Gary caught her before Ann fell. His grasp held other things than were absolutely necessary to keep her from falling.

"I told you this outfit could be touched. What do you think of this?"

Gary knew this question called for an answer, but it called for a careful answer. He did not want to tell what he was thinking right then.

"I like it. I also like that it is touchable."

"Well, then you can touch."

So saying, Ann took Gary's hand. She pushed him backwards a little. They joined each other in the big chair in front of the TV. They resumed the affectionate communications in which they were engaged when Ann had told him about her new dress.

Ann sat there curled up on Gary's lap. Ann suddenly started talking about the article. Ann said, "For some strange reason, it just occurred to me I am not properly prepared to discuss birth prevention in our article. I do not know anything about the mechanics of it. I have never had any experience. I observed at college-in the parked cars and in the dormitory-that there were some girls who were acquiring that kind of experience. I never got acquainted with any boy with whom I thought I would want or enjoy that kind of an experience, until now."

Gary, being surprised at the turn of the conversation, suddenly realized Ann was asking him if he had obtained any of that experience. Gary was puzzled. He was in doubt as to what Ann had meant when she had said "until now."

Gary decided he had better not ask. "There is nothing wrong with me. I am not abnormal. I started off in life without any money. I was a workaholic. I never got acquainted with girls. I will have to confess girls always scared me. Until I saw you around the office I had not even seen any lady whose company I thought I would enjoy. You must have observed that even with you I did not do anything which indicated I had noticed you were a very pretty lady. I did not know what to do. I did not know how to do anything. You were always so busy and business-like. So was I."

"We were not that busy."

"Until this assignment came along I was scared of you. I realized I could use this as an opportunity to get to know you. You must have noticed I was a little slow and clumsy in starting to talk to you even about this article."

"How could I be so frightening?"

"I have also observed men and women in parked cars and elsewhere, obtaining the type of experience you have mentioned. I know such things do happen. I have the same amount of experience you have. I have not thought I would want that kind of experience with any woman I saw. Even you did not make me think that way. I do not know what you meant by 'until now.' I am not going to ask."

Ann realized Gary was asking a question she was not prepared to answer. She did not answer. She did not know how the words 'until now' had come out. She had not thought about saying them. She did say, "I am glad. I am glad you have had no experience. I am glad I have not had such experience. I am glad neither of us has had such experience, until now."

Gary again noticed the words "until now." He decided he did not want to know why she was using those words.

They resumed the posture and affectionate activity in which they had been engaged when Ann had started talking about "experience."

Again Ann, without moving away from Gary or moving her head off of his shoulder, asked, "What do those men and women who I noticed having experience do to avoid having a baby, or do they just take a chance?"

Gary, without changing his position either, answered, "I understand there are different kinds of equipment and medicine available that are supposed to prevent conception."

"Do you mean the device you mentioned as a protection from conception and AIDS, and birth control pills?'

"I was surprised when I saw those devices for sale in a package hanging on a hook in a convenience store. Later I saw them in a supermarket drug department. They were there along with toothpaste and a whole variety of other things people buy and use. As I said, I have had no experience."

Ann said, "There are pills for the woman to take. The devices are for the man to use. Why are the devices for sale at the supermarket without a prescription or anything?"

"Their use is not illegal. There apparently is a demand for them."

Gary was wondering about where this conversation was going. He did not know how to stop it as long as Ann kept asking these questions. She could not be as ignorant as she seemed to be by the questions she asked. He asked, "Didn't they teach you some of these things in health class or homemaking class or physical education classes when you were in high school?"

"I suppose they did, but I did not like discussions of this subject. I did not listen. I do not remember much that was said. Do you remember anything you learned in school about this?"

Gary answered, "I do not remember that these things were even mentioned in class when I was in school. The boys did some talking about it. I never knew if any one of them knew what they were talking about. I think they were just bragging a lot of the time."

Ann then asked, "When there is so much risk, why does anyone undertake such kind of a experience? Is there some benefit, or is it some great exciting sensation or some compelling instinct or feeling?"

"Ann, you certainly ask a lot of questions I have never thought about. I certainly do not know the answer to that one. There must be some strong appeal to both the man and the woman, or there would not be so many children born out of wedlock or, for that matter, so many born in wedlock. If there was not such an appeal to both, abortion would not be needed."

"I wonder how much of that is just curiosity."

"Love must have something to do with it, too."

Ann curled up a little tighter into a ball on Gary's lap. She was quiet for a while. They renewed the affectionate communications they had been having off and on all evening. After a while Ann said, "We are writing on birth prevention when we know little about it nor why people take a chance. Perhaps we should find out something about it before we write something stupid."

"Just how do you propose we get educated on this before we do anything more on the article?"

Ann answered, "When you go to the supermarket to buy prepared food and other things, do you read the labels on the cans or packages? There is a lot of information put there as to when to use, how to use, and a lot of other things. Was there such information or instructions on the devices you saw in the supermarket?"

"I don't know. I suppose there is, but I never looked."

Ann leaned back to get a good look at Gary's face. She said, "We could find out. The supermarket is open all night."

Gary laughed and said, "You are always the researcher. Intellectual curiosity will get you in trouble some day."

"No, expanding one's knowledge is the key to progress."

"If you want to conduct some research tonight, that is probably the only place where we could learn much at this hour. If you want, we can go now."

It did not take long for Ann to throw a jacket over her blouse to conceal that it was as tight as her skin and revealed everything. She reached for Gary's hand. She pulled him out the chair and out the door of the apartment.

When they arrived at the supermarket, Ann was more hesitant to proceed than she had been in the apartment. She was pleased to see there was only one clerk and almost no customers in the store. When they found the pharmacy department, Ann was relieved to see there were no customers there. It did not take long for them to find the section where there were many different brands of the devices they had discussed. Gary looked at some of the boxes. They all had pretty pictures of men and women acting affectionately but properly. Ann looked at some of the boxes. None of them had much printing on the outside. They did not described the purpose of the contents or how they were to be used.

Ann said, "Probably the instructions are inside the box. In an aspirin box there is always a little printed pamphlet showing recommended uses, warnings, etc. I suspect if there are any instructions, they are placed on something in the box. I would guess the manufacturers want a warning there some place. They probably want to disclaim liability."

Gary replied, "We will have to buy a package to find out. I have no idea which kind we should buy. I guess we will have to be arbitrary and pick one out. I think

I will take this one as it is the most expensive. There might be more information in the higher priced packages."

Ann looked sternly at Gary. She warned, "If you buy one of these, you know you are buying only for research. But do not put it on your expense account."

"Why not if it is only for research on our article?"

"I do not want anyone to know what kind of research you and I are doing tonight. I am a little embarrassed. I am not going through the check out counter with you. That check out girl may have thick glasses. She may have never seen me before. She may never see me again. I do not want her to look at the package, then look at you, then look at me, and draw any incorrect conclusions about what we are going to do. I will buy some toothpaste and meet you outside."

Ann turned and left. Gary proceeded to the check out counter alone. The check out girl put the box in a sack, said nothing, and gave Gary his change with a small smile at him, which may have meant nothing or "have fun."

Gary met Ann outside the supermarket. They did not say much as they returned to Ann's apartment. As they approached the apartment building, there were three little steps to go up to the first floor level. Ann raised her foot to climb the small stairs. She found her slacks were so tight she could not bend her knee or lift her leg up. She had never climbed any stairs while wearing these slacks. She had only walked on the level and gone down those stairs.

Gary saw Ann's small struggle. He immediately understood. He laughed, handed Ann the package they had purchased for research, reached down, and picked Ann up in his arms. He carried Ann up the steps. At the top of the stairs, Ann did not try to get down. She continued to hold on to Gary with both of her arms around Gary's shoulders. Gary did not try to put Ann down. He continued to carry her to the apartment door.

Ann handed Gary her key. She held on tighter while Gary loosened one hand to unlock and open the door. Gary handed the key back to Ann, kicked the door open, and after going through the door, kicked the door shut. He carried Ann to the big chair before the TV, where he turned around and backed into the chair and sat down, still carrying Ann. Ann placed the package on the table besides the chair as she kicked off her shoes into the middle of the room. She curled up on Gary's lap again as they had been positioned several times earlier that evening.

The room lights were not turned on. Neither tried to turn on any light. Some light came through the windows from the street lights outside.

The affectionate but quiet communications between them resumed. Each was the aggressor part of the time. Each responded to the aggression. To Ann's surprise, she began to breath more heavily, which was something which was difficult to do in that tight blouse. She almost gasped for air as she said to Gary, "I cannot breath. This blouse has suddenly become too tight. Please unzip it."

Gary fumbled about the back of Ann's neck with one hand until he found the zipper tab. He pulled the zipper all the way to the bottom. Gary discovered the zipper came apart at the bottom. Gary did not try to reconnect the bottom of the two zipper sides. He just left the blouse completely open at the back but still on in front and over Ann's arms. Ann did not try to change the situation.

Gary soon discovered by feel what he had earlier concluded by sight. There was nothing under that blouse but Ann. She did not seem to resent Gary's hand softly exploring up and down her bare back. Gary put his hand on her back near her shoulders and under the blouse. He used that grip to draw Ann closer to him. There was no room to bring her closer.

Then Ann said, "These slacks are getting awfully tight, too, but do not unzip them. I will loosen them a little at the waist."

Ann reached around her back, found the zipper on the slacks, and loosened the zipper a little way. She did not push the zipper down to lock it in place.

As Gary's free hand explored farther, the zipper on the slacks slid further down. Again, Gary verified by feel what he had decided by sight. There was nothing under the slacks. Ann did not seem to resent Gary's exploration.

Ann said, "You are naughty."

Ann pulled Gary's shirt tail out from his trousers. She reached under his undershirt. With her left hand she explored up and down Gary's bare back. Ann used her grip to pull Gary even closer to her although that was not possible.

Neither withdrew their hands. Both used their hands to keep their proximity close and the snuggles continuous. There was neither resentment nor change of position. Occasionally Ann pulled her face back, looked at Gary, smiled, and then returned to the communications they had been having. Occasionally, Gary also pulled his face back, looked into Ann's eyes, smiled, and returned to the affectionate activity in which they had been engaged.

Talk was not necessary. None occurred. The exploration by hand continued.

At one time Ann was so quiet Gary thought she must have gone to sleep. Perhaps she had. Gary was also so quiet and relaxed that Ann could well have concluded Gary had gone to sleep. But neither slept.

When Ann got a little heavy, Gary shifted his position a little but not his hands. Ann also shifted her position some but not her hands. Ann then quietly whispered, "I cannot explain it. Please do not laugh or ask me to explain. I feel I do not want to be alone. Will you stay here the rest of the night with me?"

The light was dim but not so dim that each could not see into the other's eyes. Ann did not blush. Gary answered, "There is only one bed."

"I know."

Each continued to look at the other. Neither said anything more. Gary leaned forward with Ann still upon his lap. He got his balance. Without moving his hand which was on Ann's back, he placed his upper hand also under Ann's blouse. He lifted Ann up a bit. He stood up. Ann moved her hands to a grasp around Gary's neck. As Gary started to walk towards the bedroom, Ann said, "Bring the package."

# CHAPTER TWENTY-FIVE

There are many times, as a person passes along the road of life, when he comes to a fork in the road. There is then an option to go to the right or to go to the left. Sometimes the choice of which road to take does not seem important at the time. Sometimes, in hindsight, it can be seen the choice of the direction to go at that fork may have affected the whole life.

As Ann said, "Bring the package," Gary realized he was at a place where he had to make a decision as to the direction he and Ann should go. He could go to the right. Gary was not sure what was right and what was wrong. Nothing in his short life with Ann seemed to be wrong. Gary had feelings of doubt. Gary could have ignored the doubt. Gary could have ignored his conscience. Gary could have followed his emotions and his impulses. He could easily have gone to the left. He was not sure of his conscience, his emotions, or his impulses.

There entered into Gary's mind and consciousness the words he had heard all his life: "Lead us not into temptation, but deliver us from evil."

The temptation was there. The opportunity was there. So was the curiosity. Gary had no problems with the "evil," if, in fact, what he and Ann might ever decide to do together could be considered as evil.

Gary did not understand what had happened this evening. The evening and the events had sneaked up on him without planning or preparation. Gary did not usually proceed without planning or preparation. Gary did not understand what Ann had meant by her two statements: "until now." He was mystified by her request that he spend the rest of the night there. He was confused by her direction to "bring the package."

Although Ann did not try to get down from Gary's arms, Gary was not sure he had correctly interpreted what Ann was either saying or wanting to do. Gary guessed Ann might be having some of the same doubts he was experiencing.

Ann also realized immediately as she had said "bring the package" that she had become so confused by the events of the evening she had disconnected her brain from her tongue. She knew she had said something that rolled out without any thought. She realized she would not have said what she had said if she had not been under the influence of something she had never experienced before. Ann also realized that when she had said "until now" twice, she had not thought about saying that, either. She also could now see she did not know what she had meant by anything she had just said.

Ann was surprised at herself for inviting Gary to stay for the rest of the night. That also came out without thinking. She wondered if those statements of hers conveyed to Gary a message about her she did not want Gary to have. She could guess at the interpretation Gary might place on what she had said, whether she meant it or not.

Ann could see when Gary leaned forward, got his balance under her weight, stood up, and started walking and carrying her towards the bedroom, that he had accepted an invitation she was not now sure she had wanted to give. Ann was a little disappointed at Gary for making that interpretation, but she guessed he could not be blamed. The disappointment was overshadowed by the pleasure involved in realizing Gary wanted her in some additional way. Ann also realized she, too, wanted Gary in some additional way.

Ann was confused. She did not know what to think about herself or of Gary. She now doubted she wanted to do what she must have in effect told Gary she wanted to do. It was not that she was suddenly concerned about what was right and what was wrong. She knew what was wrong. She did not feel that what they had experienced together so far was wrong.

There came to Ann's mind the words she had heard all her life: "Lead us not unto temptation, but deliver us from evil." Ann realized she had been playing with temptation and curiosity. She was confused by what might be evil.

Ann now realized it was time to make a quick decision. She was not sure what decision she wanted to make. She was sure of what her decision should be. She did not know how, after she had made the decision, she should act or what she should say to Gary to change the interpretation she must have given to him.

Mutual confusion and doubt existed. When Gary heard the words "bring the package," he stopped. He did not return to the table besides the big chair in front of the TV where the package was waiting. He looked into Ann's eyes. He thought there was either doubt or fear there. He was not sure of what to do or say.

Ann looked into Gary's eyes. She did not see any aggression or compulsion to proceed. Ann thought she saw a little uncertainty, perhaps even reluctance. Ann did not release her grip around Gary's shoulders. Gary did not release his grip and hold of Ann.

How long it took for these thoughts to pass and these emotions to become controlled by the mind would have been difficult to measure. Ann was light and graceful. Gary was big and strong. A time arrived when Ann did not seem as light as she had seemed when Gary picked her up. Ann's arms seemed to be carrying more of her weight.

Without a word being said, Gary turned, walked by the little table near the chair in front of the TV, and stopped. He did not reach for the package. Ann also did not reach for the package. Gary turned again, backed into the chair, and sat down with Ann still in his arms. Ann silently thanked Gary for making her decision for her.

Ann curled up in Gary's lap, placed her head upon his shoulder, shivered a little, and said nothing.

Gary noticed Ann as she curled up in his lap and placed her head upon his shoulder. Gary bent down, placed his lips on Ann's forehead, and said nothing.

Gary did not try to raise the zipper on Ann's slacks. He did not know how to place the two zipper ends together on her blouse, so he just put his hands on her back and pulled her closer to him. Ann did not try to close either of her zippers. Ann reached again under Gary's undershirt near his back and shoulders. She pulled Gary as close to her as she could.

It had been both a long and a very fast evening. Time passed beyond where each of them would have customarily separated for the evening. Nothing was said about that by either.

Both being very comfortable with each other, the needs caused by exhaustion overcame the feelings caused by emotion. The rest of the night passed without either knowing the world was turning.

# CHAPTER TWENTY-SIX

As the darkness faded away, the street lights went out. A different kind of light came into the room. The restlessness of the light and restrictions of movement by the closeness of the two of them in the chair brought each Ann and Gary to consciousness, not simultaneously and not quickly or suddenly.

As awakening occurred, Ann turned her face up to Gary's face. They met halfway. They repeated the silent conversations of the previous evening. Ann was the first to speak, "I am glad. I am glad for what I did and did not do until last night. I am glad for what you did and did not do until last night. I am very glad as to everything I did and did not do and what you did and did not do last night. The evening was not planned that way. Such an evening and what was done and was not done was not even contemplated. I am glad. I will never forget or regret one single instant of last night.

"Gary, thank you for making the right decision for me and for you and for us. I will let you make some other decisions for me and for you and for us again some other day."

Gary was afraid to ask what Ann meant.

Gary knew he had to respond to Ann's open expressions. He still was being careful as to what he should say, still remembering what he had said last night without thinking and the slap. Gary did not respond directly. He did say, "You and I started out together on a business basis, with the intention of being adversaries and co-authors. Some time ago I noticed, and I am sure you noticed also, that I quit thinking of you as an adversary and started thinking of you as any good healthy man might think of a good healthy, pretty, smart, and considerate woman."

"Go ahead, Gary. I am listening."

"I hope, Ann, I did not misinterpret. It seemed to me you stopped thinking of me as an adversary. I am not sure what thoughts of yours replaced the adversarial position. I do not want to guess. I can hope, but I will not tell my hopes out loud right now, at least."

"I would rather listen to what you might say than interrupt. Go ahead."

"I, too, Ann, did not plan last night or contemplate what happened. I, too, am glad for what did not happen last night. I will also not forget or regret any part of it.

"I never realized how exciting and relaxing falling asleep in each other's arms might be. It was a comforting situation. It is too bad people put a nasty connotation on 'sleeping together.' Sleeping together in the same chair, as we did, was not naughty. It was not anything anyone should feel ashamed about. I feel good and exhilarated because of it."

"Yes, I agree, Gary, but do not tell anyone we slept together. They are sure to misunderstand and think we did something that only married couples should do."

"It cured me of any feeling that you and I are adversaries."

"I am glad we never became adversaries. I am glad we are not adversaries. I am not sure what we are to each other, but whatever it is, I like it.

"Ann, I have read about the feelings of togetherness. I cannot explain, but while we were so close in this chair and actually fell asleep in each other's arms, something came to me from just being close to you. I felt as if it flowed from you to me."

"I have that feeling, too, Gary. It is wonderful. Do you suppose the feelings we might have shared could have been so great if we had actually gone to bed together, used the device, and learned whatever would result from that?."

"How could that have been better?"

"In doing what we did I have only the feeling of exhilaration."

"If we had done the other, I do not know what physical feeling I would have received. I think the physical sensation would have been fleeting and be gone by now. I have no feeling of guilt, fear of having made you pregnant, fear of people thinking that my feelings for you were the result of a shotgun marriage if something had gone wrong."

"I am the one who should be grateful. I am the one who suggested it. I am the one who would have been taking a chance on being pregnant. I am the one who would feel guilty. I feel great right now. My present thoughts and feelings right now cannot help but be better than my feelings would be now if we had finished what we almost started to do."

Gary said, "Yes, I feel the same."

"I am happy for togetherness. I know that togetherness has given me a feeling of well-being and excitement I am sure will last a long time."

"That may be more than one should want or have. The rest would be confusing. There is a time and place for everything. We are not at that time and place."

Now it was Ann's turn to speak-if taking turns was what they were doing. She now interrupted before Gary had finished. "A new day has come. It is a new day in our thoughts, feelings, and actions towards each other. It is also a new day at the office. It is time to return to reality."

Ann started to get up out of Gary's lap. He would not let her go. He held her for a few more gestures of affection and silent communication of their feelings to each other. Ann did not resist.

"If the memory does not annoy you, you may use my father's electric razor. I noticed just now you do need to use it."

So saying, Ann placed, for the last time this morning, her lips on Gary's lips. She turned, got up, picked up her shoes from where she had kicked them when they came back from the store, and danced away. The open back of her blouse was swinging. Her exaggerated movements were aimed right at Gary. Ann went into the bedroom. She closed the door. She did not need any help with her zipper this morning.

# CHAPTER TWENTY-SEVEN

On the twenty-eighth day a draft of their article was complete. Ann and Gary each reviewed it. They made some minor changes and corrections. Late that day neither could find anything more they immediately wanted to change.

"Ann, we have reached the point we knew we would have to reach in thirty days. We did not think we could cover the subject in that time. We have covered a lot more than I thought we would. We could do more. There can always be something added. Yet, there could never be complete coverage. Each day we think about the subject and the article, we will make changes. I hope we have done a credible job. I think it is time to finish and deliver the article to Burner."

"Yes, I think we can finish now. I think it is a pretty good article. Burner may never read it. He might not like it. All those ideas, discussions, and adversarial arguments you and I have had might go to waste and never be known. I do not want this just buried in a file. I want Burner to use it."

"I feel the same. This article is not mine. It is not yours. It is ours. It is a product of our minds and our life together."

After making the final changes they had agreed upon and making up a clean copy, it was late Friday afternoon.

"Let's go together to deliver this to Burner. He might want to talk about it. He should know, if he does not, that it is our mutual work."

Ann carried the original copy. They walked together to Burner's office without any conversation. Fred Burner was in, but, as probably could have been expected, he was on the telephone.

While Burner continued his telephone conversation, he looked at them. He pointed to the calendar on his desk which showed the reminders for the day. They could see the reminder which showed "Article on survival and prosperity due today."

Burner kept on talking to someone on the other end of the telephone. He raised his hand that was not holding the telephone. He placed his middle finger and thumb together to make a circle. He nodded his head, smiled, and pointed to an empty space on his desk. Still talking, Burner waved a short good-bye.

Ann and Gary walked out of Burner's office and down the hall. They had feelings other than one of accomplishment. They both felt let down. They both had the sadness that their enforced working together so closely was now over.

Without talking, they wandered out of the building together. They went to a little place where occasionally they had danced to the juke box. Gary put a couple of coins in the juke box. Ann pushed the buttons for a slow but cheerful tune. Without a word, Gary put his arm around Ann's waist. They danced. They said nothing.

When the coins ran out, Gary said, "Tomorrow is Saturday. We ought to take the day off and drive out of this city into the countryside we may have helped to survive. We wrote about it together. We have not seen it together."

Ann responded, "I am tired."

"I am tired, too. I do not blame my tiredness on working on this article."

"Are you going to blame our tiredness on sitting up together all night?"

"I am giving that credit for a different kind of relaxation which left us both weary when it was completed."

Ann said, "Whatever it was, I liked it then. I like it now. Meet me at my apartment at ten tomorrow morning."

Without waiting for an answer, Ann turned, walked out, got into her car, drove home alone, and took a long hot bath.

As Ann soaked in the tub, thoughts that pleased her came to her mind. They were of Gary. She liked to place happy thoughts in rhyme. She prepared, in her mind, a rhyme that fit what she was thinking. When she got out of the tub, she wrote what she had thought. It was

> Is Gary Just Playing A Game?
> Does He Want To Change My Last Name?
> I Will Have To Be The First One
> To Start Something To Get This Done.
> I Will Take My Very First Chance
> To Heat Up Our Luke Warm Romance.
> I Will Get Him To Clearly See
> That He Does Want To Marry Me.

Ann's happy thoughts were there as she drifted off to sweet dreams.

When Ann left Gary, he grabbed a ready-made sandwich, got into his car, went to his room, and without taking off more than his shoes and tie, laid down on his bed. He lost track of reality with Ann on his mind and with happy feelings.

# CHAPTER TWENTY-EIGHT

When Gary arrived at Ann's apartment the next morning he was a little early. The door was partially open. As he approached, Ann called out, "Come in. Make yourself comfortable. I will be with you in a minute."

Gary walked in. He sat down in the big chair which faced the TV. Gary again lost track of reality.

When Ann came out of the bedroom, she stopped when she saw Gary there obviously at peace with the world. Instead of feeling insulted that meeting her was so unexciting that he would fall asleep, Ann felt flattered. She knew Gary was so comfortable with her that he could completely relax and be entirely at ease.

Ann, too, felt that same comfort with Gary sitting quietly in her home. Such comfort was, she knew, a precious commodity. Ann did not want to interrupt it. There was no other chair for her to use to do the same thing. The thought occurred to her to crawl right into that same chair with Gary. The temptation did not seem practical or comfortable right then. She decided to make a lunch for the day's adventures.

No sooner than had Ann reached into the refrigerator for whatever she was going to use to make a lunch than Gary was standing there beside her.

"I apologize for falling asleep when I was looking forward to seeing you and spending the day with you. You have made my life so comfortable that the situation I felt caught up with me. I am surprised at myself. Just being with you has been so exciting I cannot understand how I could have relaxed so fast. I like the kind of combined comfort and excitement that I have when I am near you. I like your companionship. I would like it if that would last forever."

Ann smiled. This was the chance she had set out in her rhyme. She turned her face up to Gary and asked, "Mr. Live, have you just proposed to me?"

Gary did not realize that was just what he had done. He also quickly understood that was just what he wanted to do someday. He had not planned it for today. It seemed that most of the things between Gary and Ann had just happened to him without plans and preparation. Gary was not used to doing something without planning and preparing. He had no plan. He did not know what to do or what to say. He said nothing.

Ann did not let the subject drop.

"Gary, if you did not mean that as a proposal, I will not be annoyed, but I will be disappointed. When you said you liked my companionship and would like it to last forever without mentioning marriage, I could have interpreted your comment as that you would like to live with me without being married. I think too highly of you to believe you would suggest such an arrangement, so I do not believe that is what you meant. That leaves only marriage as what you intended. If it was your intention to just live together, I am disappointed in you. I can answer right now. I will not do that."

Before Gary had a chance to say anything, Ann said, "If that was not your intention, you will notice that I did not say no. You will also notice that I did not say yes. You would not expect me to answer such an important question without a warning to let me think about it, would you?"

Again not waiting for Gary to say anything, Ann said, "Survival of the earth will depend upon smart and caring children to replace smart and caring parents as much as survival depends upon avoiding the things that damage or hinder survival and prosperity."

"Yes."

"I will answer your proposal, if it was a proposal, but not right now. Let us go for the ride we planned. We can consider things together during the rest of today."

"I am ready."

"Excuse me, I want to get my walking shoes."

Gary was silent. As Ann turned towards the bedroom, she said, but not loud enough for Gary to hear, "You asked me when we started discussing Burner's memo, 'Is this a joke?' I can answer now. For me, it has not been a joke."

Ann left the room. She went to her little desk in the bedroom. She pulled out her note paper. She wrote:

Dear Mother:
I want you to be the first to know. I have found the right guy. You will like him. You will adore your grandchildren.
Love,
Ann.